T0196344

finding andie

Marsha Bjerkan

authorHOUSE®

AuthorHouse™
1663 Liberty Drive
Bloomington, IN 47403
www.authorhouse.com
Phone: 1 (800) 839-8640

Published by AuthorHouse 09/22/2017

ISBN: 978-1-5246-9759-4 (sc)
ISBN: 978-1-5246-9758-7 (e)

Library of Congress Control Number: 2017910599

Print information available on the last page.

This book is printed on acid-free paper.

Contents

Finding Andie

It was a cold, blustery day the first part of January, 2004. I was curled up on my sofa reading the Milwaukee Journal .The fire roared in the fireplace as the wind blew fiercely outside. I was temporarily living in Milwaukee, Wisconsin conducting leadership training for a large insurance company. As I read the newspaper on my day off I saw on the front page an article about forty-four puppies rescued off of an Indian reservation outside of Milwaukee.

Greta was the only dog I had had in my adulthood. She was an eight week old German shepherd mix rescue puppy. I remember looking at the ten rescue puppies and zeroed in on Greta because she immediately waddled over to me and sat down on my foot and looked into my eyes. Well, she immediately captured my heart. Picking her up, I kissed her on her nose and then looked over at the director of the facility and said, "I definitely want this little one to go home with me!" That was on a cold day in December, 1982. I tucked Greta in my down jacket to protect her from the cold as I walked to the car. That was the beginning of our life together. We had a marvelous life playing together, loving each other and spending enormous amounts of time just cuddling. She was such a well behaved and special dog to me. Eventually after eleven wonderful years together her health rapidly declined. It was so difficult to see this once vibrant dog begin to slow down and barely be able to walk a few steps. I knew it was time to help her make the next journey; the one journey I didn't want her to make because she would no longer be with me. I contacted the vet and told him it was time. He knew it was time because I had been to see him with Greta a number of times hoping and praying for a miracle. It was a terrible day when I took her in for her last visit to the vet and her last day on earth. Tears were streaming down my face as I walked in and held her tightly, feeling her, loving her and remembering all of the years of love she had given me. She had made my life complete. I held her as the vet gave her the injection that would eventually stop her heart. I felt my heart stop as she was slowly leaving the world. I whispered in her ear, "Honey, please wait for me at The Rainbow Bridge because I will see you there and we can go to heaven together." I thought at the time that there was no dog that could ever replace her. Greta and I had been inseparable and a large part of my heart shattered that day with the loss of Greta. When I walked out of the vet clinic, I felt lost and lonely. That had been nine years ago and I had not thought about getting another dog in all of those years since.

I am not sure what triggered a feeling in me that day in Milwaukee, reading about the rescued puppies off of the Indian Reservation… but something made me want to explore it further. Several of my friends I talked to that day about these puppies encouraged me to get another dog. They kept telling me that after nine years, I needed to give love to another rescue puppy and provide that dog with a safe, caring and loving home. I thought about their words and explored why I was feeling something after reading this article. I was nervous because I questioned whether I could love another dog like I had loved Greta. I was anxious about whether I could take care of a dog and provide it with the love it deserved. I pondered these thoughts and anxieties the rest of the day.

Finally, that night, a good friend of mine, Lori, called me again about the rescue puppies. She asked me if I had given serious thought to exploring the possibility of getting another dog. I told her that all afternoon I had been consumed with those thoughts along with so many questions. Lori said, "Marsha, you know how to give love. You gave Greta love, care and devotion and she gave it back to you. You rescued her and she lived a vibrant life. What if you hadn't rescued her? Who knows what kind of life she would have lived. It may not have been a home filled with any love or care for her. A rescue puppy deserves a chance of living a life that is filled with care, love and compassion given by its owner. There are too many rescue puppies that never get that chance. You need to give yourself a chance to love again and give a rescue puppy a chance to live a wonderful life!"

I really thought about Lori's words. Maybe it was time to open my heart again. Maybe it was time to love another dog. Maybe Greta was looking down on me from The Rainbow Bridge and praying that I would rescue a puppy and give her the same life that I had given to her. I wrestled with my feelings all afternoon and finally decided that it wouldn't hurt to visit the Humane Society that evening and take a look at the puppies.

It was early evening when I entered the Humane Society. The article said that people could come by that evening to view the dogs, but anyone who was truly interested would have to wait until the next day to ask for one. It was amazing at the number of people swarming in with me to see these puppies!! I had no idea the attention it had received from the community and the draw from the people to find one sweet puppy for them. I walked down the aisles and looked into the cages to see the puppies. My goodness, there were so many and they were all looking at me with eyes filled with fear; fear of where they were and fear that they would always be alone. My heart broke for all of them. Looking at them took me back to when I had found Greta. She had been a rescue puppy that, I am sure, had that same look of fear in her eyes. I had forgotten about that. I had rescued her and given her a loving home. I knew just then, I needed to help one of these puppies. I needed to give one a home so that it would never feel fear again!

I kept walking the aisles and then I looked over at this one puppy in a cage. It was huddled close to the back of the cage looking out at the people wandering through. I stopped and sat down to look at this puppy closer. It was a black Labrador mix with sad eyes. I said, "Hi, sweet thing. You look so pretty with your big brown eyes and black ball of fur." She looked up at me and slowly got up and started walking to the front of the cage closer to me. When her nose was touching the front of the cage, I gently put my hand up for her to sniff it. She sniffed my hand for the longest time periodically looking up into my eyes then back to sniffing my hand. She eventually sat down and began licking my fingers. When she looked up at me, I saw these beautiful big brown eyes staring at me. She seemed comfortable being with me. Her expression was so gentle and loving. I know I was feeling comfortable being with her. After about thirty minutes, she laid down, again close to me at the front of her cage and her eyelids started to get heavy. She was getting tired. Her eyes opened a little more and looked directly into my eyes. It was almost like she was saying, "I like you. I am getting tired, but I hope you come back tomorrow," I knew she was growing weary so I said to her, "My sweet thing. I will come back tomorrow morning early and when I do, I am going to take you to your forever home. Your gentle heart and loving eyes have stolen my heart. I will take care of you for the rest of your life. Rest now and I will be back. I promise."

When I left and got into my car, I sat there for the longest time thinking about what I had just experienced with this rescue puppy. I was amazed by the feeling I had when I had been with her; her beautiful brown eyes looking up at me, how comfortable she had been licking my fingers and just being close to me. I had not felt a tug or love in my heart for any dog since Greta who had died nine years earlier. I felt that tug now for this puppy. Yes, I would be back in the morning to claim this little one to be my own and to give her the love and care she deserved and that I so wanted to provide to her.

I could hardly sleep that night because of my excitement in going back to the Humane Society to claim my sweet rescue puppy. I tossed and turned and finally I decided to get up, dress and get over there. I arrived long before the facility opened. I didn't want to take any chances of losing my puppy I so connected with. There had been so many people looking at the puppies the night before and it concerned me that one of those folks may have fallen in love with my rescue puppy! There was no way someone else was going to claim her. She was mine! When I arrived four hours before the facility opened, I was surprised to see there were six people ahead of me in line! I prayed that they weren't there to claim that seven week old black Labrador I had met the night before. It was cold outside, but that didn't matter to me. I waited and waited until finally they opened the doors. When the doors opened those six people ahead of me pushed forward as I tried to inch my body through the group to reach the puppy I had fallen in love with. I managed to escape the other six people and ran madly to that puppy's cage. She was still there!! She saw me and her tail started wagging. That was her signal that showed me she remembered me. I looked at her and said, "My sweet thing, I came back!!! I told you I would!"

I knew that this dog was different. She wasn't Greta, but Greta and I had had our own love and life together. Finally, nine years after Greta, I understood and accepted that there can be more than one love in your life. I had found another dog that could provide me with the love I so wanted as I would provide her with the love, care and devotion she deserved. Our life together would be filled with fun, love and adventure. Our life together; those words sounded so good.

I walked up to the director of the Humane Society and said," I want that puppy", as I pointed to the adorable black ball of fur with the beautiful brown eyes staring me in the face! After I signed the release papers, I raced to her cage, opened it up, and she ran into my arms. Have you ever known what it feels like to fall in love at first sight? Well, I felt it immediately. We were destined to meet and begin our journey through life together.

I picked her up and tucked her in my down jacket, strolled off to my car with this amazing smile on my face that could have lit up the world. My life was full again and it was all because of this little ball of black fur that had looked at me with those beautiful brown eyes.

Andie, Meema and Me

After I picked up my sweet rescue puppy and before I headed for my home in Kansas City, I spent two days trying to decide on a name for her. I spoke to several of my friends and there were names tossed around like Iggie from <u>Fried Green Tomatoes</u> to Annie. Finally, I decided on the name Andie. I had always like that name because I liked the actress Andie McDowell and I had worked with a woman by the name of Andrea who went by Andie. It just seemed like the right name, I thought, for my sweet little girl. So, two days after I rescued her, it was official. Her name was Andie. Andie and I spent a good deal of the first two days learning where to potty and where NOT to potty, like NOT in the house. When we first arrived at my apartment in Milwaukee, she explored every inch of the place and discovered she loved to take the end of the roll of toilet paper and carry it throughout the house. She was discovering new things that she had never been exposed to before. Given the fact that she was only seven weeks old, she had many new things yet to discover! At the end of the week, my training assignment ended and we were headed back to our home in Kansas City. I was ready to get back to my family and friends; yet, I had decided not to tell my family about my "new addition" until I was settled in. The ride home was pretty easy. Andie sat in the passenger seat and just stared out the window and frequently glanced at me probably thinking, "Mommy, where are we going?" It was fun for me to have her with me. She was my dog and I was relishing every moment I spent with her. She was my love and now very much a part of my life. Our journey together was just beginning. I smiled all the way home!

It was a Saturday morning, the day after we had arrived and I called my Mom, who was also called Meema by my nephews and niece. She and I had always been so close especially after my father had died suddenly of a heart attack six years prior. I was wondering how she would feel about adding a new puppy to my life and her life. I will never forget that day my Mom, Meema, came up to my house to see my new addition to the family. When she walked in, the little black ball of fur with beautiful brown eyes came tearing out of the family room headed straight towards Meema, who was just walking in the door. Andie crashed into her legs and rolled over on her back waiting for Meema to scratch her tummy. Meema looked down at Andie and then looked up at me and said, "I can't believe you got a dog, Marsha! A dog is a big responsibility." I told Meema that I knew she was a large responsibility, but I had fallen in love with her the minute I laid eyes on her. It was her big brown eyes that had looked straight into my soul and heart and said, "I like you. I want to be with you for a really long time." Who could walk away from that, knowing that this little creature lassoed my heart and would change my life forever? Meema just shook her head and then without thinking she bent down to scratch Andie's tummy. I believe that was the beginning of their loving journey with each other.

Andie became an integral part of my life, and then she became my life! When I thought about what I was going to do every day, at the top of my list was Andie. When I ran errands, I always took her with me. I loved how she rode in the car. Her head was hanging out the window with her ears flapping and her tongue wagging to and fro. What a sight she was. It was like she was shouting out to the world how much she loved life. It was all an adventure to her. Every day; every event; every person she met, she exuded the love of life that so many people wish they could capture and hold on to themselves. She did it effortlessly and with such abundant joy.

I felt so fortunate to be a part of her life and share joy she embraced daily. Because of her zeal for being alive, she made me feel the same way. I had a lighter step as I would cruise through my day. When I had to go to work, I would love on her, give her a treat and tell her to be good and I would be back shortly to take her for her daily walk. Now, I wouldn't say "walk" instead I would spell it out. W-A-L-K. If I didn't spell it out, she would hear that word and go wild with excitement.

I made it a point of taking her and Meema to the dog park four times a week. I thought it was important to have her get to know other dogs and owners. Meema and I loved watching Andie play with the other dogs. At first she was timid. She was so little that she looked at these big dogs with a bit of reluctance. Over time, though, she looked forward to visiting the dog park. When we would be within one mile of the dog park, she KNEW where we were going. She would begin to wag her tail and bark at the top of her lungs because she couldn't wait to get there; to get out of the car and greet and meet all of her friends.

She was quick to become comfortable with the dogs, the owners and romping around the park. It was a 20 acre park so we walked the parameter of it until we reached the lake. She was a bit tenuous when it came to wading in the water. She would dip her paw in and then retreat it immediately. It took her the longest time to wade in up to her belly. That was about as far as she ever went. Even though Lab's are known to be water dogs, my sweet Andie was not one of them. Meema and I laughed at how she was so reluctant to go any farther into the lake. That was not, nor would it ever be something she enjoyed doing. So check off throwing a Frisbee out into the lake for her to retrieve. That Frisbee would simply sink to the bottom of the lake while Andie was watching from the shoreline next to Meema and me. It didn't matter to me. She was kind and gentle to dogs and people and that was most important. I wanted her to understand love, care and compassion.

Andie and I spent a good deal of time with Meema. The second most important love in Andie's life outside of me was spending time with Meema. Honestly, there was this unspoken love and commitment between the two of them. When I would say, "Andie girl, do you want to go see Meema?" she would leap up and literally go pick up her leash. I am not exaggerating! We would drive over to Meema's house and Andie would jump from the car and bound toward her front door. Meema usually was waiting for us. When Andie would be walking up the steps, Meema would open the door and Andie would fly inside with her tail wagging its way in. Meema would look at Andie with her gentle eyes and embrace her with a loving hug. I've often thought about that first time she met Andie at my house as she bounded toward my Mom, crashed into her and rolled over on her back begging Meema to scratch her tummy. To think that my mom had even questioned why I had gotten another dog!

Now let's fast forward to the times when Andie visited Meema's house. Meema couldn't wait to see Andie. My, oh my, how love changes things in such a wonderful way. There was so much love between the two of them. I was sometimes in the background because Meema and Andie were so into each other. Andie became a fixture at Meema's house. When I had to go out of town on business, Meema would take care of Andie. She said she didn't mind and actually loved the company. Meema was free about feeding Andie "human food" especially potato chips. When Meema and I would sit down to have lunch, Meema would sneak a potato chip to Andie, hoping I wouldn't notice. Of course, I did! I would say, "Mom, you shouldn't be feeding her those chips! She is going to begin to beg all of the time when we are eating." Of course, my Mom's response would be, "Oh, Marsha, she will be okay. What is one little chip?"

This routine went on until mom started having challenges maintaining the house. It was difficult for her to keep up with cleaning the house, doing the laundry and just overall house and life maintenance. I spoke with my brother and sister about this and they agreed it might be better if we moved Mom into an independent living facility. We gathered together over at Mom's house one afternoon to talk with her about this and get her thoughts. We loved her so much and just wanted her to be happy and not have the worries of maintaining a house. When we talked to our Mom we told her that we loved her and wanted the very best for her. We talked to her about moving into The Forum, an independent living facility. She would be able to live on her own yet have the amenities of events offered to the residents, dining facilities and a place that would care for her. We talked it over with Mom about moving from her home of 56 years. At first she was reluctant because she loved her home; the home where she and Dad had raised their three children and shared love, laughter and relationships with their neighbors. She struggled thinking about this change of moving, but in the end, she knew it was the right thing to do. She wasn't able to take care of the house anymore. It was too much; yard work, housework, all of the things you need to tend to being a homeowner. It was her time to enjoy independent living at a facility that catered to people like my mom. As it turned out, it was a joyous time when we moved Meema into The Forum.

Once settled into her apartment, I took Andie over to visit Meema. My gosh, you would have thought they hadn't seen each other in years! Andie couldn't get enough of Meema and vice versa. They loved, cried and hugged each other for so long. I just sat back relishing in the moments of my mom and my dog loving each other. It was priceless and unforgettable.

Andie and I visited Meema every day at The Forum. A new chapter began. It wasn't Andie bounding up the steps of Meema's house, now it was Andie bounding through the doors of The Forum. She knew that once we were through the doors, we had to wait for the elevator to take us to the second floor. Once we exited the elevator, Andie pulled me to Meema's door and began scratching to let us in. Andie knew Meema would be there ready to love on her. Isn't it precious to see the purity of unconditional love a dog gives? Andie showed that love to Meema day in and day out. Remembering the day Meema first met Andie and the look of shock on her face when she saw that little ball of fur running towards her to now when Meema is opening her arms to love on her "little girl" makes me smile. What a difference Andie made in Meema's life.

Andie and Our Visits to The Forum

Andie and I continued our daily routine. We would wake up together and love on each other basking in the glory of a new day. Andie knew our routine after getting out of bed. We would go downstairs for breakfast, read the paper (really, I would read the paper while Andie chewed on her toys). After I showered and dressed, Andie's tail would begin to wag. At first, it would gently swing back and forth until I would ask her, "Do you want to go see Meema?" Then, her tail would be swinging back and forth a mile a minute while she barked at me. She knew where we were going. She knew who we were going to see. She knew it was her Meema that was waiting for her.

When we pulled into the parking lot of The Forum, Andie could hardly contain herself! She was crying for joy and was pawing at the door to let her out. I would say, "Honey, let me park the car and then we will go in and see Meema." Well, that brought more crying and barking because she wanted out of the car and so wanted to go see her Meema.

I would get out of the car with Andie right on my heels. I would grab her leash and she pulled me in the front door of The Forum. When we walked through the common area, the residents would greet us, or rather, would greet Andie with their sweet smiles and genuine feeling of love for my little girl. Over the course of time since Mom had been living at The Forum, the residents had gotten to know Andie very well. There were residents who actually sat in the common area waiting for my sweet girl to burst through the door. So many of the folks would walk up to her and pat her on the head and whisper sweet nothings in her ear. They had grown to love this black ball of fur. She was so gentle with the residents and always willing to sit next to them while they kissed her and told her how glad they were to see her. This had become a part of our daily ritual when visiting Meema. The residents needed to see Andie and spend time with her. Many of the residents did not have family that visited with them and they were lonely. Andie eased that loneliness and brightened their day. They looked forward to their visit with my little girl.

It touched my heart every time we walked in the front door of The Forum. It also broke my heart to see some of the residents that I knew had no family members or friends who visited them. Andie helped them with their journey through life. She made their lives happier by looking forward to her visits. She gave them purpose for getting up in the mornings and walking down to the common area knowing that Andie was going to be there to love them.

It gave me joy to see the interactions between the residents and Andie. It always touched my heart to see the impact Andie made on them and as well, the impact they made on Andie and on me. They brought joy to our lives with their kindness and their desire to spend time with this little black ball of fur that knew nothing but love and the easy way she loved everyone she came in contact with.

After a while, Andie would look up at me as if I knew what she was thinking. She was saying, "Mommy, it's time to go see Meema! Let's go now, okay!" She would tug at her leash as she ran to the elevator that would take us to Mom's second floor apartment.

Always, when the elevator stopped on the second floor and the door opened, Andie flew down the hallway to Meema's door. She would take her paw and tap on the door and immediately Meema would open the door, bend down and give Andie kisses and hugs and say, "Honey, I have been waiting for you!"

It was our beautiful life together; Andie, Meema and me. We didn't have to be doing anything special. Just spending time together;

just the three of us was special enough. It was all we needed. Every day, every minute that we were together was precious and so memorable. Sometimes we would take a walk down the hallway to the dining room where they allowed dogs. We would have lunch and chat with the other residents. Other times, if the weather was nice, all three of us would take a walk around the grounds.

No matter what we did, we did it together. We could overhear some the residents talking to each other saying "Aren't those three so sweet together? They are lucky. I wish I had what they have. I wish I had someone to come see me every day." It made me feel so good because we were special together. Andie, Meema and I did love each other and loved spending time together. It also hurt my heart knowing that some of the residents didn't have anyone visiting them. I am glad that Andie and I took the time to visit with those residents that so looked forward to my little girl bustling through the front door every day. Hopefully, we brought joy and love to their lives, at least, for a while. Everyone deserves to be loved and to know there is someone who cares for them.

Meema

One day in July, Andie and I went to visit Meema like we always did. Andie was pulling me through the door of The Forum and raced to the elevator anticipating the greeting she would receive from Meema when we reached her apartment door and she would open it and hug and love on Andie.

We reached her door and knocked on it. We waited and when Mom didn't open the door, we knocked again. After a minute, I was getting worried so I took out the key to her apartment and opened the door. Andie ran ahead looking for Meema. I was right behind her wondering why Mom hadn't greeted us at the door like she normally did.

Andie and I immediately went into the bedroom and saw Mom lying down with her eyes closed. I paused for a second fearful that she was sick. I sat down next to her and said, "Mom? Mom, are you okay?" Her eyes slowly opened and turned her head slightly to look into my eyes. "Marsha, I don't feel good. I think I need to go to the hospital." She said in a whispered tone. I asked her what hurt and she said that she had chest pains. I immediately dialed 911 and told them to come immediately. I told them that my Mom was having chest pains and seemed very fragile. I was scared. I was scared for my Mom. I was scared for Andie who was sitting right next to me with her ears back and her tail tucked between her legs. It was almost like Andie knew something was wrong and she was worried as I was worried.

The paramedics arrived and checked Mom's vital signs. They then put her on the stretcher and loaded her into the ambulance to transport her to the hospital. Andie and I were right behind them getting into the car to follow them.

On the way over, I called my brother and sister and told them what was happening. They were going to meet me at the hospital. I was shaking out of fear for my Mom and wondering what was happening to her! It was hard to focus on driving, but I finally made it to the hospital. I turned to Andie who was sitting in the passenger's seat with a pensive, forlorn look in her eyes. I put both of my arms around her and told her that Meema loved her and that I loved her. I asked her to be good and stay in the car for a while so I could go check on Meema. Andie turned her head and looked right into my eyes and it was as though she was saying, "Please let Meema be okay, Mommy."

I ran into the emergency room entrance as the paramedics were bringing in Mom. I asked them how she was doing and they said that they needed to keep her for observation. They said that they were concerned about her heart. At that moment, my heart stopped. I asked them if she was going to be okay and they said that they were doing everything possible to help her. My brother and sister walked in just seconds after my conversation with the paramedics. I brought them up to speed about what had happened when Andie and I arrived at Mom's apartment and that she had been having chest pains. All three of us just hugged each other and prayed that our Mom would pull out of this.

The doctor on duty found us about thirty minutes later and told us that they were taking Mom up to the Cardiology floor. They had a room ready for her. The doctor told us that his concern was that her heart beat was weak and they needed to perform tests on her to check the health of her heart. He assured us that he and his team were doing everything possible to take care of her and to find out her prognosis. He told us it would be several hours before they had any results from the tests they were going to take. I asked him if we could see her for just a few minutes. He hesitated and then told us that only for a few minutes. She was tired and needed her rest.

We walked into her room and saw her lying in the hospital bed with her eyes closed. I quietly walked up to her and reached my hand out to hold her hand. Her eyes slowly opened and she looked at me and then turned her head to see that my brother and sister were on the other side of her bed. "Well, what is happening?" she asked. "Mom, you are at the hospital. Do you remember anything about when Andie and I came by your apartment to see you today?" I nervously asked her. "Well, kind of. I remember you sitting next to me on the bed. I don't remember anything after that." She said with a shortness of breath. I went on to explain to her that the doctor was going to run some tests to find out what was happening. My brother and sister reassured Mom that everything was going to be fine. She was in good hands with the doctor and his staff. All three of us, almost in unison, said how much we loved her. We said that because it was going to take time to run the tests, the doctor told us that we should wait a few hours to find out the results. Mom was looking at us with a blank stare. She was shaky and scared and told us that she wanted to go home. I held her hand tighter and said, "Mom, let's first find out what the tests show us." With reluctance she nodded her head. We hugged her with all of the love we had and told her we would be back soon.

After leaving her room, my brother, sister and I walked out to the parking lot. We talked for a long time about Mom, her health and our fears about her heart. We loved our Mom so much and didn't want anything to happen to her. She was our life. She definitely was my life and Andie's life!

I told them I needed to take Andie home and that I would meet them back at the hospital in three hours.

I got in my car and looked over at Andie. I told her that Meema was going to be in the hospital for a while. I started to say something else and realized nothing was coming out of my mouth. Tears were streaming down my cheeks and I bent over to hug Andie. I was so scared. I didn't want anything to happen to my Mom. She was my life. She was Andie's life. All three of us were one. We had done everything together for the past five years. I couldn't think of not having Mom in my life, not having Meema in Andie's life. As I hugged Andie, I prayed to God that he would help Mom. He would make her better. I prayed from the depths of my soul that God would help. I prayed for Andie because she had no idea what was happening. She knew something was going on and she seemed nervous and anxious. I knew she was feeling my emotions and seeing my tears. I kissed her and told her that Meema would be fine.

We drove home and walked into the house with heavy hearts. I sat down on the sofa and Andie climbed up next to me and put her head in my lap. We sat there for a long time clinging to each other, holding tightly to each other and I was praying to God the whole time.

The phone rang and I jumped up to answer it wondering if it was the hospital. "Hello," I said anxiously. "Yes, is this Marsha Sawyer?" "Yes, it is" as I hesitated a bit. "This is Doctor Hughes. I think you need to come back to the hospital as soon as possible. We got the test results back and I want to talk to you about them." I told him I would be right there. I called my brother and sister and relayed what the doctor had said. I looked at Andie and told her that I would be back as soon as I found out what the test results showed for Meema. I gave her a kiss and a warm hug and then left.

When I arrived at the hospital, the doctor was waiting for my brother, sister and me. We all came in at the same time and the doctor asked us to sit down. All three of us held each other's hands as we waited to hear what the doctor was going to share with us. He gave a heavy sigh and said reluctantly, "Your mother's heart is weak. We have put her on medication to help strengthen her heart. I am concerned because of her age and the condition of her heart valves.

We are going to keep her here and monitor her heart to ensure that the medication helps." I was the first to speak up. "Doctor, do you think that she may have a heart attack." He replied, "There is always that chance, but we are doing everything possible for that not to happen." We just sat there. I stared at the doctor with eyes filled with fear. He went on to say, "Your mother is being well taken care of by my staff and by me. I know this is very difficult for you to hear, but truly, we are doing all we can to stabilize her heart. I will keep you abreast of any new developments. Right now, your mother needs to rest. I am so sorry to have to share this news with you."

We didn't move for a long time. We just stared at the doctor and hoped for a miracle. He said again, "I promise that I will keep you up to date on your mother's progress. All we can do is monitor her, let her get rest and continue to take her medications. I will call you later tonight to give you a progress report." We thanked the doctor and then went downstairs to the cafeteria to talk. We were all concerned about her health, her heart and her progress. All we wanted was for her to get better and have her back in her apartment enjoying life.

I told my brother and sister that I was going home to take care of Andie. Since the doctor had my number, I knew I would get the phone call. I told them that if I heard anything, I would call them immediately. We left the hospital with so many concerns swirling through our minds; concerns for our mother, concerns about if the medications would work; concerns if she would have a heart attack and concerns about if she would make it back to the apartment.

I walked into the house and Andie was waiting anxiously by the door. She normally would be laying on the sofa, but not this time. She knew something was terribly wrong. She knew it had to do with Meema. She knew. I lay down on the floor and hugged her close to me. I told her everything the doctor and said and then told her how much Meema loved her. Andie's ears perked up at the sound of Meema's name. Andie scooted in closer to me almost like she was telling me that she loved Meema and she wanted her to be okay.

We went to bed early that night and just loved on each other, holding on to each other for dear life. At about 11 p.m. the phone rang and I jumped up to answer it. It was the doctor. He paused and then finally said, "I am so sorry to tell you this. Your mother had a massive heart attack just a few minutes ago. We tried our hardest to bring her back. I am so sorry. I am so very sorry. We couldn't save her. She died."

At that moment he said she died, a part of me died along with her. I cried like I had never cried before. I told him through my tears that I was driving to the hospital. I called my brother and sister and had to tell them the news. We were all in shock and grieving over the loss of our Mom. the mother who had always been there for us; loving us unconditionally and knowing that we were her life. She had loved her life and loved raising her three children, proud of the adults we had become. She had loved Andie with all of her heart and soul. Without my Mom, without Meema, I was lost in grief and my whole life had been turned upside down. How would I get through this? How would Andie feel knowing that she would never see Meema again. She didn't know because she still thought Meema was alive and that she would see her again with Meema waiting by her apartment door with her arm stretched out ready to give her Andie girl a big hug. Andie had no idea what had just happened.

The next week was a blur for me. It was agony to plan Mom's funeral and to know that this was final. I just went through the motions with a heavy heart and a lost look in my eyes. I know Andie was disturbed. I could see it in her every movement. She was anxious and I knew she wondered why we hadn't gone to see Meema.

After the funeral was over and several days had passed, it was time for me to take Andie over to Meema's apartment. It was time for her to know; to know that Meema wasn't there anymore. Oh my, I grieved over how Andie was going to react.

The next day, I put Andie in the car and drove over to The Forum. When we arrived and parked the car, Andie's tail was wagging back and forth with the anticipation of seeing Meema. It broke my heart to see how excited she was. We got out of the car and Andie was pulling at her leash to get in the door of The Forum. The residents were sitting in the common area and this time, they were quiet and subdued as we walked in. Some of the people had tears in their eyes knowing what had happened to my Mom. I think they were crying for Andie who did not know she would never feel Meema's arms wrapped around her or feel her kisses on her face. They looked at me and told me how sorry they were for the loss of my Mom. Andie, not knowing anything, bound for the elevator that would take her to Meema's apartment. When we arrived at Meema's apartment, Andie scratched on the door so excited for Meema to greet her and give her the normal hugs and kisses before we ever entered the apartment.

I looked down at Andie and said, "Andie girl, there has been a change. You will soon find out and I am sorry for this. I am so very sorry." I unlocked the door and Andie burst through and ran to the living room and looked around expecting to see Meema, she then ran into the bedroom and ran in circles looking and anticipating Meema to come out of the bathroom and bend down to kiss her sweet Andie girl. Andie was confused. She ran back into the living room, then the kitchen and back into the bedroom. She did this several times and then finally sat down and looked up at me with a bewildered look on her face.

How do you explain death to a sweet innocent dog? How do you explain that my loving girl would never feel Meema's arms wrapped around her? She would never feel the kisses that Meema constantly gave her every time she saw her. How can you explain that to a dog that had only known Meema as a vibrant, caring woman who unconditionally gave Andie her love and compassion? You can't; I couldn't. I sat down next to Andie in Meema's apartment and explained to her that Meema was in heaven and that she was watching over us. She would always be there for us in spirit. She would always love us as we would always love her. Andie looked at me with sorrowful eyes. Somehow I knew she sensed that there had been a significant change that happened that affected my sweet girl. After a long time of sitting on the floor and wrapping my arms around her, I got up and said, "We should leave Andie girl. We should go home." I took her leash and began walking towards the door and halted because Andie was still sitting on the floor and wouldn't move. I tugged at the leash and said again, "Honey, it really is time to go." She wouldn't budge. She was planted there and would not come to me. She was not looking at me; instead she was looking around the apartment. Her head was turning right and left and her eyes were seeking out the Meema that she had loved her whole life. I knew she was confused and hurt because Meema wasn't there to love her. I let the leash go and sat down beside my little girl and held her. I told her how much Meema had loved her. I cupped my hands around her face and looked deeply into her eyes and said, "Meema will always be with us, honey. She will always be looking out for us." After about an hour, Andie got up and slowly walk towards the door. Andie turned her head to look back into the apartment and then looked up at me with sorrowful eyes. We left quietly and got in the car to head home.

Healing in Colorado

The next three years were difficult for both me and Andie. In our own ways, we grieved for the loss of my mother. The days melted away with me going through the motions of life and taking walks with Andie. You could see in Andie's personality that she wasn't the same excited dog that loved life. There was something that caused her to be lethargic and sad. Whenever I said the word Meema, her eyes would shine brighter and her ears would perk up. I decided it was healthier for her if I didn't mention Meema's name so much. I think it hurt her in the end because she was expecting to see Meema. I didn't want to give her false hope.

Instead, I told her how much I loved her. I made a special effort to spend more time with her. We went to the dog park more frequently so she could play with her furry companions. We went on longer walks to give us more time together. We even went out to my sister and brother-in-law's house in Colorado to hike the trails. My sister knew how much my heart needed mending, so she told me to take as much time as I needed to heal. She told me their house in Colorado was waiting for us.

I took her up on her offer. I thought new scenery would be healthy for me as me as well as Andie. I packed the car and headed west. We spent three weeks at their place. Every night I would read the hiking trail book to Andie and I would ask her opinion about the trails I was deciding on for our next day's adventure. (as if she knew what I was talking to her about!)

We would get up early every morning and I would have chosen a trail that I thought we would both like. Well, lo and behold, Andie was the leader of the pack. I drove us to the trailhead and she would jump out of the car with her tail wagging and her spirit full. We ended up hiking an average of ten miles a day. She loved every minute of our time together on the trails. We would pack a lunch and stop half way through our hike to rest, eat and enjoy the scenery. We didn't rush our walks. We took our time and simply enjoyed each other's company and the beautiful mountains that surrounded us.

It was so therapeutic for me. I could visibly see the life coming back to Andie. Her spirit was back because at night, she would run through the house with a zeal I had not seen since Mom died. She would leap up on my lap and literally put her front legs around my neck and lick my face over and over. It made my heart feel so good. I had so wanted her to be herself again after Meema's death. It had been a long time since I had seen Andie this contented. This had been the best idea my sister had suggested to me. I wanted Andie to be happy with life and ready to move on her journey with love in her heart.

The three weeks in Colorado went quickly. Every day we hiked and explored the different trails and at night we relaxed at home with a fire roaring in the fireplace and the two of us snuggled together. That time was magical and healing for both us. It helped that we had each other. It was an adventure for us to learn that we both loved hiking. Actually, Andie truly was the leader. She pulled on the leash as we walked the many miles through the mountains enjoying the changing of the season with the aspen trees turning their beautiful colors. The hiking healed me. I was beginning to be happy with life again, and I think, in turn, helped Andie. Truth be told, Andie had helped me with my grief. I knew that Meema was there with us. Maybe we couldn't see her, but I knew I felt her presence surrounding me every day. It helped to feel that because I knew I wasn't alone. It still was Meema, me and Andie, just in a different way.

When we left Colorado and drove back home, We were well on our way to healing from the loss. It had been a magical time with my sweet Andie. It was the beginning of a new chapter in our life's journey.

Andie's Certification

One afternoon, while walking Andie on our usual route, I stopped to talk to one of my neighbors. In the course of our conversation, my neighbor told me she had trained her dog to be a certified therapy dog. She loved taking her dog to nursing facilities, hospitals and hospice locations to visit and comfort the residents and patients. I asked her what it took to have a dog become a certified therapy dog. She explained from the get go that the dog had to innately be gentle dealing with people. The dog had to be approachable, loving to others, and able to work alongside other therapy dogs. I knew Andie was a great candidate because she met all of those qualifications. My neighbor said that she had certified her dog through Pets for Life, which was known to be a very reputable organization. She, as well as her dog had really enjoyed the training experience. She told me to check it out if I was serious about the certification process

I thought this would be good for me and Andie. Hadn't Andie already help ME out of the deep grief! Yes, she had! And Andie had loved visiting Meema in the independent facility, as well as visiting with the other residents that we would greet walking into The Forum. Maybe by becoming a therapy couple, it would help both of us. We could visit the residents like we had when we would go see Meema. Andie had always loved interacting with the people we would see when visiting Meema. Maybe this would be a good activity for both of us; giving the residents joy and ultimately having Andie and me receive joy from those visits.

The next day, I called Pets for Life and inquired about enrolling Andie in therapy training. They told me I could apply for a "pre-test" orientation that would demonstrate what was involved in the testing process. I told them to sign me up!

Two days later I arrived ten minutes early because I was so excited about this opportunity for me and Andie. They told me that the "pre-test orientation" would only involve me, not Andie. They wanted to talk with the owners and let them know what to expect with the testing and qualification process. When I walked in, there were twenty people sitting at the table exhibiting the same level of enthusiasm that I had. We were all eager to get started.

The staff took us through the testing process that would be performed on our dogs. The dogs had to be able to sit, stay, lie down, avoid other dogs, maintain their composure if they heard loud noises and be able to maneuver around wheelchairs. I was wondering at the time if Andie would be able to meet all of the criteria. She had never been in an environment where there were loud noises and she also took her sweet time laying down! I was hoping and praying she would pass the test because I knew she would relish this experience of meeting people who needed love, plus, I definitely wanted to be a part of that experience with her.

After I left, I went home and told Andie that she was going to become a therapy dog and help people. I went on to say that we had to practice some techniques so that she would be ready to go through the testing process. So, every day we practiced all of the techniques she needed to perform at a perfect level. I am sure she wondered at times why I was so focused on how she sat, how she laid down, how she had to avoid other dogs. Andie, also, had to be able to pay little attention to objects that were in front of her, whether it was a toy, a ball or a wheelchair. I wanted her to do her best so she would pass her pre-test. After two weeks of intense practice, I thought she was ready. I called Pets for Life and scheduled our pre-test.

The day of the pre-test arrived. Would Andie pass? I was nervous! I entered the office where we were going to take our pre-test. Andie was at ease, but my palms were sweaty. The trainer asked us to walk in and sit down in one designated area. One of the instructors approached us. Andie and I were instructed to do a series of exercises – walk around in a circle and then turn around and walk back. The instructors looked to see if we were at ease walking together. Next, they asked us to walk around with wheelchairs, walkers, and lots of noise to test how Andie dealt with the turmoil. To my delight, Andie handled that situation superbly. I was so proud of my little girl, Andie, had performed.

The only thing we needed to work on was having Andie lay down. It took some work because by now Andie was nine years old and had gone through surgery the year before to repair a torn ACL. Overall, the instructor said that Andie had done a good job with everything except lying down quickly. I told the instructor that we would continue to work on that.

When we got out to the car, I hoisted Andie up in the passenger seat, slid into the driver's seat and immediately hugged her. I said, "My sweet girl, you did a fabulous job! I am so proud of you for how you performed. We just need a little work on how you can lay down quickly and then, Andie, you are as good as gold." As we drove home, Andie's head was hanging out the window with her ears flapping and a smile on her face. I think she knew that all was right in the world.

For the next two weeks, I worked with Andie on all of the techniques we needed to perform to qualify her as a therapy dog. I'd take her out for walks and purposefully walk next to another dog to coach Andie on simply walking on and not paying attention to the other dog. That was one of the techniques we had to master; being focused on walking and not on playing with another dog. The Pets for Life instructor was adamant about this. She told me that in order for Andie to qualify, it was important that she not be distracted by other animals. There'd be other therapy dogs at the facilities and that all therapy dogs had to be trained not to run and play with other animals. The primary focus for therapy dogs was interacting with the residents. We practiced and practiced until Andie had perfected this technique.

We continued to work on the other techniques, then zeroed in on the one that needed the most work; lying down. Andie had taken too long to lay down when we'd gone through our pre-test. Andie and I practiced daily on having her lay down immediately on command. She was an older dog, so it took her a bit longer for her to lie down quickly. I was determined to work as long as it took for her to master this technique. After two weeks, Andie was doing better with lying down. She seemed more comfortable and more confident with this. I thought she just might meet this challenge and become a therapy dog.

The day came. We walked into the room where the dog trainers were administering the tests. Would Andie pass? We began the testing process. Andie did a good job of avoiding other dogs, sitting, staying, and not being unnerved by loud noises or wheelchairs swirling around her. As we were approaching the end of the test, the trainers asked me to have Andie lay down. I felt like it was a forever moment until I looked at Andie and very calmly said, "Honey, lay down please." Then I felt like it was an eternity after I spoke those words as I looked at my little girl.

As I looked down at Andie, those big brown beautiful eyes looked up at me and seemed to say, "Okay, I will be okay with this," and she immediately lay down in front of me. I lowered my face to hers and gave her the biggest kiss! She had done it! She had mastered all of the techniques.

I looked at the certification staff and they were smiling from ear to ear. The instructor said, "Well, Andie passed with flying colors! Congratulations, she passed all of the tests and now she is moving on to the final test. Andie and you will be visiting a facility and will actually walk around and meet residents with the Director by your side to see how she performs in a real situation." My heart was bursting with pride! Andie did it! She was on her way to being a certified therapy dog.

I was confident Andie would be just fine with this final test. I had tears running down my face because of the joy I felt. I was so proud of her and what she had accomplished. She looked up at me and I swear she was smiling back at me! She nudged my leg and seemed to be telling me, "Mommy, we did it! Let's go home now."

We walked out to the car and we got in. I looked over at Andie and cupped both of my hands around her face and gave her a huge hug and kiss. I whispered to her, "You are my sweet therapy dog, Andie. Together, we are going to bring joy to residents who need love and care.

Andie's Final Test

It was a beautiful day in October with the leaves changing colors and the smell of fall in the air. Andie and I were scheduled to meet the Director of Pets for Life, as well as, an employee of The Forum, the facility where my mother lived for two years. We were going to walk through the halls, greet people, and observe how Andie conducted herself.

As we were driving over to the facility, I kept telling Andie she'd ACE the certification. I really believe she was listening to every word I said to her. She frequently gave me this look like she was saying, "Mommy, I'll be just fine. Just you wait and see!" Then, she placed her paw on my arm and left it there for the rest of our drive.

As we turned into the parking lot, her tail began wagging wildly. I think she knew where she was and that she thought she was going to see Meema. Andie was so excited she began to scratch the door. She was telling me to let her out, now!!! She pulled me to the front door with absolutely no hesitation! As we entered, there were several residents sitting around the common area. I walked up to each resident and introduced Andie. One resident said that she didn't like dogs However, it was only five minutes and that very resident said, "I remember a black Labrador I had as a child and I loved that dog. I am not sure what had happened in her life that changed her mind about dogs, but she seemed to dig back into her memory on that one special dog that had touched her heart. She even walked up to Andie and gave her a gentle pat on her head.

A gentleman walked up to Andie and gave her a pat on the head and a kiss on her cheek. He shared that when he was a child, his father raised Labradors as bird dogs. As he continued to love on Andie he elaborated on his story about all of the techniques his father had used to train the dogs.

The Director of Pets for Life met me a few minutes later and took Andie and me to the assisted living area. She wanted to observe Andie's interactions with the residents as well as how I interacted with them. I was also introduced to Steve, an employee with the facility. He would be walking with Andie and me during our visit.

Steve, the employee, said that he would like for me to visit with the residents. I took Andie to the common area and walked up to each resident. One resident, Margaret, who was munching on popcorn said, "Andie, do you want some popcorn?" Andie didn't even try to nibble at a kernel and Margaret said, "I can't believe she doesn't like popcorn, but what a sweet dog she is!" Margaret lowered her hand to Andie's head and gave her a soft, loving pat on her head, saying over and over again, "Good girl…what a sweet girl." Andie drew closer to Margaret and gave her a loving nudge on her leg. There was another resident, Jill, who seemed to have a forlorn look on her face until I introduced her to Andie. Her eyes sparkled, a smile appeared on her face and her hand gently extended out to touch Andie.

Steve then took me down the hall to see Donna. He said that she had raised and shown bulldogs. She was a dog lover. Steve knocked on her door and said, "Donna, I have a special friend I want you to meet." Donna slowly got up from her bed, secured her walker and came to the door to welcome us (actually, she was more interested in Andie than the rest of us).

She said what a beautiful dog Andie was. She slowly sat down in her chair and asked Andie to come let her pet her. Andie with her loving eyes looked at her and walked up to let Donna pet her. Donna then began sharing about her life and her love of dogs as she continually stroked Andie's head saying, intermittently to Andie, "You are such a good dog. Stay with me so I can love on you."

We stayed with Donna for twenty minutes and right before we were leaving there was another resident coming down the hallway with her walker. She stopped in front of Donna's room. Her eyes lit up as she waved and smiled at Andie. Andie was making a difference in their lives and actually, they were making a difference in ours.

We left Donna's room and walked to a secluded area to review the visit. The Director and Steve said that Andie was a very good fit for this facility. She was well behaved, seemed to connect with the residents and was accepting of the love and pats on the head she received.

So, she passed!!!! Andie was an official therapy dog ready to embark with me on our new journey.

That visit to the facility that day brought back such loving memories of my mom and the visits Andie and I had made daily. I had seen people who I'd met when visiting Meema. Interestingly enough, they remembered Andie and me! The accountant of the facility came up and greeted me with a gentle hug and a kiss to Andie. She said that it had been too long since we had visited. She noticed that Andie was grayer, but still the wonderful loving dog she remembered.

The therapy sessions at this facility were going to be so gratifying. I could just feel it.

I left with an extra bounce to my step. I could feel the smile on my face. After I put Andie in the car and settled in the driver's seat, I turned to her and told Andie how proud I was of what she had accomplished. I honestly think she understood what I was saying because she turned her head and looked right into my eyes as if she was saying, "Mommy, we are going to be a good therapy team. I love you."

She then rested her head on my arm, closed her eyes and gave a contented sigh as she drifted off to sleep.

Our Journey Continues

After Andie became a certified therapy dog, we made it a point to ask for our visits to be at The Forum where Meema had lived her last two years. I requested The Forum because of the fond memories of our visits to see mom and other residents. Before our first official visit, I put the Pets for Life bandana around Andie's neck and told her we were going to work! It was a memorable time for the two of us. So many of the residents were receptive to petting and loving on Andie while I asked them about their lives. It was so rewarding that I began journaling our experiences.

We'd been visiting the residents every Friday afternoon for two months. I noticed that several of the same residents were always in the common area when Andie and I arrived. As we walked toward them, they'd say to each other, "Andie's here!" I walked up to each resident and said, "Andie wants to say hello. Is that okay?" The overwhelming response from all of them was a resounding yes! While visiting each person, Andie would gently place her head in their laps and let them slowly extend their hand out to pat her. Andie was patient with each resident resting her head and letting them pet her for as long as they wanted. She seemed to know that she was there to make their lives better.

The residents' reactions to their excitement when they saw Andie brought back memories of when we had visited Meema. When Andie and I visited Meema at The Forum, Andie couldn't wait to reach my mom's apartment. Always, when my mom would open the door, she had this unique smile when she saw Andie. She would say, "How's my little girl, honey? I love you!" My mom would bend down, wrap her arms around her neck and give her a loving kiss. You could actually see the love they felt for each other by the looks in their eyes. Andie's tail would wag a million miles a minute.

It was just like the residents who waited for Andie to visit them at The Forum. The residents had the same look in their eyes when they saw Andie walking toward them with her tail wagging wildly. It was like Andie was sharing the same love for them that she shared with Meema.

For me, I was sharing the same journey that Andie was experiencing. She and I both had loved our Meema with all of our hearts. Meema had brought us joy and unconditional love. She was there to embrace us and provide us with love, care and tenderness.

Andie and I visited our Meema every day of her life at The Forum. It was a ritual I treasured and one that I was vigilant in keeping for two years until the day Mom died.

The importance of Andie's and my journey with certifying her to become a therapy dog and specifically choosing The Forum was to honor my Mom and to honor the residents who, perhaps, didn't have family or friends that visited.

There were many times when we would be visiting Meema and she would say that a particular resident never had visitors. Meema would ask if Andie and I would visit that resident. Well, of course, we wanted to! Mom would take us to the resident's apartment and we would sit and listen while the resident talked and smiled at Andie. Many times those residents would open up their hearts and share pieces of their lives that had been so dear to them; perhaps events in their lives they normally didn't share with everyone. Andie made the difference. She approached them with a simple love and unconditional trust. She would lay by their chair and let them lay their hand on her head while they shared their life's stories.

Each of us has the opportunity to make a positive difference in others' lives. Andie's journey as a therapy dog made a significant difference in my life. She taught me unconditional love, the art of patience and how to love, care and always help another person.

Andie's journey continued with me by her side. Every day I learned more about love and giving through the eyes and guidance of my Andie. Our journey continued with an awareness of how the two of us could make a positive impact on others by listening to their stories and providing our love and support as they, too, continued their journey through life.

It had been a magical journey for Andie and me because of the residents we had grown to love, the excitement in their eyes when they saw Andie walk through the door. I never imagined how rich and rewarding this journey with Andie, my therapy dog, would be. It changed my life and I know if Andie could talk she would echo my sentiments.

Spotlight
Carol and Carol

Andie and I were at The Forum on our normal day and time that week. We had been spending time visiting several residents who were confined to their room. They enjoyed the break in their day to smile and show their love when they saw Andie. Some residents had lost their sight, but that didn't deter them from hearing Andie's feet padding across their hardwood floor and sniffing at their hands as they extended them out to her. They still had the same type of smile and that same love that radiated from them when they touched my little Andie girl.

After our individual visits to those residents, Andie and I gravitated back to the common area. We always did. It was a place where many residents gathered as well as visitors who came to spend time with their loved ones. We were visiting with one of our "regulars", Bev, when I heard a voice from behind ask "Do you mind if I pet your dog? " I turned to face where the voice came from and there was a woman about 40 year's old sitting next to one of the residents. I got up from the floor where I had been sitting with Andie visiting with Bev. I told Bev I would be back.

I walked over to the woman and said, "No, I don't mind at all if you pet my dog. Her name is Andie and she is a therapy dog. My name is Marsha." The woman in kind responded, "My name is Carol. A therapy dog! That is so wonderful that you are both doing this for these folks. It really means so much to them because dogs are innocent. They only know love and they give that to each of these people." I thanked her for saying that. Carol went on to say, "My mother and I are here visiting my grandmother. " As she spoke those words, her eyes were squarely focused on her grandmother. "I come to visit her as much as I can. You see, I live in Rhode Island so it is a bit of a journey to fly to Kansas." As she continued to share with me, it was abundantly apparent the special connection between granddaughter and grandmother. Carol said that her grandmother was so very special to her. She started sharing about how she was born in Kansas City, but because of her mother's job, they had moved to Rhode Island when she was in high school. During her childhood years, she and her grandmother were inseparable. They would cook, bake, take walks, play cards and just spend time doing nothing. No matter what they were doing, it was the togetherness they most relished. It was a difficult adjustment moving away from her grandmother who was her role model and best friend. What made it easier were her grandmother's frequent visits to Rhode Island. She actually spent several weeks during the summer with Carol and her mom and always extended stays over the holidays. I listened with a keen ear and sense of love for their relationship. Carol looked at me and apologized by saying, "I'm sorry. I have not formally introduced you to my grandmother. Her name is Carol. I was named after her." I believe the sun moved from outside the building to inside because there was a brilliant radiance surrounding Carol when she introduced me to her namesake.

I asked her what she did in Rhode Island. She told me that she was an acupuncturist for both pets and humans. She told me how gratifying it was to help heal them from their pain. She said that for ten years she had been a vet tech. It was rewarding because of the pets and owners that she had befriended throughout her career. I asked her why she had decided to change careers and move into acupuncture. She said that as a vet tech, there were too many times when she had to assist with putting down an animal because of a terminal illness and feeling helpless in the process. She wanted to be in a position to help animals overcome illnesses and obstacles to continue to enjoy life. She felt that acupuncture was an eastern medicine that blended well in our western society. She had been an acupuncturist for several years and during this time she had shared several stories about how her work had helped and healed animals that perhaps may not have been so fortunate. It was fascinating to listen to her. Clearly, her enthusiasm was heard in her voice and shown on her face as she talked about her journey in her career. Carol said, "I wanted to make a difference. I wanted to help animals and people and acupuncture has been my calling. I have treated animals that have been abused and have worked with them to a point where they have felt safe. I have treated animals that have been diagnosed with a serious disease and have been able to help them either back to health or help them with relieving the constant pain of that disease, at least for a while. I feel I am helpful in what I am doing now versus helpless in what I did as a vet tech. I love working with the animals and their owners. I spend considerable time with my patients which have resulted in strong relationships formed. "I was enthralled with our conversation and with the commitment and love she had for her job, the people she helped and most of all for her grandmother. You see, her grandmother had been listening in on our conversation and the whole time her grandmother was smiling ear to ear. I could tell how proud she was of her granddaughter.

All the while as Carol and I had been talking, Andie was lying next to Carol with her legs splayed out in a relaxed position. Her eyes had frequently been looking at Carol and then back to me. It was almost like she understood our conversation. Carol had periodically placed her hand on Andie's head as she shared her story. It was a comfortable and easy conversation. I felt like I had known her for years because of the ease in which she shared her life with me.

It was getting late and dinner was about to be served to the residents. Carol looked at her mother and then at her grandmother and said, "Well, grandma, we better go so you can get something to eat. We will be back early tomorrow so we can spend all day together." Andie heard the word "go" and stood up, looked at me in a knowing way assuming we were leaving too.

I got up; put my coat on and told Carol and her mother that Andie and I would walk out with them. I walked over to her grandmother and gave her a gentle squeeze on her arm and said, "You have a remarkable granddaughter." Carol, her grandmother, looked at me with a twinkle in her eyes and said, "Oh, I know, I know."

I began walking to the elevator behind Carol and her mother. I hadn't noticed until at that moment that Carol didn't get up and walk out with us. Instead, she wheeled herself to the elevator. I realized she was wheelchair bound. We rode the elevator down and left the building together.

Before we parted, I told Carol how much our conversation had meant to me. She smiled and said that it had meant the same to her. She wished us well and again shared how special our therapy was to the residents.

As we parted ways, Andie and I slowly walked to the car as Carol's mother was pushing her daughter's wheelchair to their car. I stopped and observed as Carol's mother helped her daughter into the car, dismantled the wheelchair and lifted it into the trunk of the car. She shut the trunk walked around the car and got into the driver's seat. As they backed out, they turned and waved at us as they left.

I reflected on my chance meeting with Carol. Remembering when she asked, "Do you mind if I pet your dog?" I got up from the floor where I had been sitting with Andie and turned to Carol and said, "No, I don't mind if you pet my dog. She is a therapy dog." From there I immersed myself in this woman who had such a love for her grandmother, a passion for her career and a zeal for life. It was her aura that mesmerized me. She loved life. I could sense it and see it. Despite the challenges she faced with her disability, it didn't deter her from embracing life and living it to its fullest.

I was humbled. I take for granted every day when I wake up. I climb out of bed and I walk to the kitchen to fix coffee. I open the door and walk outside to retrieve the paper. I put Andie's leash on for her daily morning walk. After Andie and I would return, I would walk upstairs to shower, change and get ready for work. I would kiss Andie good bye and walk out the door to get in my car. I would drive to work with not a care in the world.

In reflecting on my life, I had taken the little things for granted. I thought I had challenges and they evaporated before my eyes when I thought about the challenges Carol had faced in her life. She faced the big things daily; maneuvering through life in a wheelchair.

Then my mind drifted off to the residents in The Forum. They were captives in their own bodies. Many had difficulties just lifting an arm much less getting out of bed to walk down the hall for breakfast. The residents had challenges day in and day out. Many had to be lifted into their wheelchair, secure their legs in place so as not to harm themselves as they wheeled down the hall. Others gripped their walker and diligently, yet carefully put one foot in front of the other working their way to the common area.

Yet, the many times Andie and I had been visiting them, not one person complained about their situation, about their challenges, about the obstacles they faced daily. No, they never complained.

When Andie and I would visit the residents every Thursday afternoon, I would say to them, "Hi, Andie and Marsha are here to visit you." Not just one time, but every time I announced we were here, overwhelmingly the residents would say in a gleeful way, "Andie's here, and where is my Andie?" They were always so happy to see us, mostly Andie! To them, they didn't have challenges. That was just life. It dealt you some difficult hands, but it was how you played the cards that made you a winner.

It gave me pause. So much so that I went home that night conscious of how I got home (I drove myself) and sat on the sofa with Andie and wept. I wept for all of the people that couldn't do the simple things every day. I wept for the residents at The Forum who had lived a productive life and were now slipping into their last chapter in life, yet, those residents were upbeat, excited about waking up every day and seeing their family, friends and even Andie and me.

I said to Carol that Andie was a therapy dog. In thinking about what I learned from her that day; her passion for life and her spirit that oozed out of her pores, she was my therapy. Without knowing, she had shown me what life is all about. It is how we deal with the challenges in our lives. We could be wallowing in our misery every day because we had a flat tire; we didn't win a running race; we ran to catch the bus and missed it.

Now, in my reflection on what I had learned, it was the depth and breadth of what was inside a person that made their life joyful. It was the positive energy and passion for life that made that person whole and alive. It was dealing with the challenges by not making them challenges. It was a part of life. They went far beyond those challenges because it didn't matter. What mattered was the love of friends, family and life. It was the fact that they were able to wake up in the morning and begin a new day.

I realized that my life changed in one day, one chance meeting with a woman from Rhode Island flying to Kansas City to visit her grandmother; her name sake that she cherished with all of her heart. She embraced life with not a thought about what she was challenged with because in her mind and soul she had no challenges. She had life. Just like the residents at The Forum. They thanked God every day when they woke up and started their day.

Life. We should never forget what the treasures of life are. It's about loving unconditionally; telling friends and family how much we love them; sharing with others unselfishly.

Life. Embrace it with all of your heart. I am now. Andie gave me that experience with Carol and understanding the love of life. Andie was the conduit between Carol and me. Carol was initially drawn to Andie not me. Andie was the gift who allowed me the introduction to Carol. Oh, the beauty of Andie, my therapy dog.

Spotlight
Clarice

Andie and I met Clarice on our very first visit to The Forum. She was secured in her wheelchair sitting in the Common Area, where most residents gather throughout the day. We walked up and knelt down beside her wheelchair. I introduced her to Andie, my therapy dog, and me. I asked her name and she said in a gentle voice, "My name is Clarice."

I told her she had a beautiful name and her lips curled up into a smile. I asked her if she wanted to pet Andie and she extended her gnarled hand toward Andie's head and with a gleam in her eyes she said, "Oh yes, I would like that very much!" Clarice asked if her name was Dandy. I said no, her name was Andie. She said Sandy? No, I said her name is Andie. Clarice had a bit of a hearing problem. If she wanted to call her Dandy or Sandy, it didn't matter to Andie and me. The only thing that mattered was having Andie give Clarice love and attention. Of course, Andie enjoyed the affection Clarice gave her. I visited with Clarice that day and every visit after discovering more and more about her journey through life.

Clarice was born in 1912 in Kansas City. She was raised in the city where her father was a milkman and her mother stayed at home to raise Clarice and her two siblings. It was an idyllic childhood where children were safe to play in the streets after dark with no threats of being kidnapped looming nearby. (My, things have changed since then!). She graduated from high school in 1929, the year of the Stock

Market Crash. She was all set to attend the local college; however, the Crash altered her plans. Her parents had lost money in the stock market crash and just didn't have the means to send Clarice to college.

Clarice ended up getting a job as a helper in a grocery store. She worked there for several years and during that time she took a couple of college courses every semester. She was determined to get her college degree. After six years of working and attending college, she was able to achieve her goal. She received her degree in education. It was difficult to find a teaching job during The Great Depression so she kept working at her current job.

One evening a couple of months later, a friend asked Clarice if she would be willing to go to a party with a friend her boyfriend knew. Clarice wasn't too keen on the idea of going to a party with an absolute stranger, but her friend convinced her that the four of them would have a good time. Clarice reluctantly agreed. Little did she know that evening would change the course of her life.

Clarice met Ben, of whom she was going to the party with as well as her friend and boyfriend. As Clarice put it, "It was love at first sight!" When Ben and Clarice looked at each other for that first time, she swore it was the Fourth of July with fireworks exploding all around them. Three months later they were married. They had three children and raised them on a small farm on the outskirts of town. Her husband worked for the government while Clarice stayed at home to raise their children. On their farm, they had several horses and dogs. She taught her children about responsibility by tasking them with feeding the animals. They learned how to balance their chores and school work. It was a home filled with love and respect for family. Clarice and Ben were role models to their children by demonstrating what a good marriage looked and felt like.

In the late 1940's, Clarice decided to get her Juris Doctorate. Now, that was highly unusual. The majority of housewives were focused on their home and family. The thought of seeking a job outside of the home much less going back to school was not on their radar screen. Ben was very supportive of Clarice's plan and helped her with the family chores to make it happen for her.

She still took care of her family as she always did. The only change was during the evenings when most people were winding down Clarice was attending college taking night classes. This journey took four years, yet at the end, she was handed her diploma! Her family was proud of her accomplishment! She took her Missouri bar exam and passed.

By this time, her children had graduated from high school and were living their own lives. Clarice decided to put her degree to use. She applied for a position as an estate tax lawyer for the government and got the job!!! She worked there for the next twenty-five years.

She was only one of two women at that time working in a department of one hundred employees. Over the years she was employed, she saw many changes primarily with the increase of women in the workforce. When she retired in 1978, the workforce looked very different. Instead of only 2% of the department's employees being women, 60% were women. Clarice truly had been a pioneer in the twentieth century.

Sadly, Ben died in 1998. Clarice mourned his death and the end of their journey together. Her children and grandchildren were by her side to love and care for the husband she lost and for the father and grandfather they lost. It was a difficult time for Clarice. She had to recreate her life without her soul mate. It took several years to push through her grief until she finally came out the other end.

Clarice had always had a love for life, was committed to her family and strong in her faith. She had led an active life with a taste for adventure.

Six years ago her eye sight began failing, her memory deteriorating and the ability to care for herself almost nonexistent. Her children were concerned for her safety and decided it would be best for Clarice if she moved to a skilled facility. They moved her to The Forum where her next journey began. She was living the last years of her life now in a wheel chair with gnarled hands, an arthritic ridden body and difficulties with her short term memory. Her daily activities consisted of sitting in the Common Area with the other residents waiting for the morning to turn into evening and then for bedtime to arrive. There were the occasional visits from her children and grandchildren, yet, they had their own lives filled with jobs and endless responsibilities. It was difficult for them to visit her frequently.

So, here I was back for my weekly visit and Christmas was five days away. Andie was at her usual spot sitting beside Clarice's wheelchair. Clarice lightly patting Andie on her head telling Andie how much she loved her. Clarice was reminiscing with me about her life. Her long term memory was solid. She remembered the details of meeting Ben, falling madly in love, raising her children and eventually, going back to college to get her Juris Doctorate. She had lived a rich full life. She had been a vibrant woman living her dreams.

I asked her what her plans were for Christmas. There was a long pause. I looked into her eyes as they began welling up and a tear slowly rolled down her cheek. I didn't ask again. As I saw that tear roll down her face and then another tear soon followed, I thought about her life, the many wonderful journeys she had taken over the years and the final journey she was on. She knew it too.

She continued to pet Andie as she had this faraway look in her eyes... I simply put my arms around her, gave her a warm hug and told her how fortunate Andie and I were to have her in our lives. She smiled and continued petting Andie.

Clarice brought joy into Andie's and my life. She had shared her story that revealed the many facets of her life, love of family and determination. Now, at 101 years old, she was winding down, growing wearier by the day.

Clarice had become my role model. She taught me to relish in my life's journey; live and love to the fullest. This is the beauty of being a "therapy couple"; learning life's lessons through the people who are on their last journey in this life. While the residents pat Andie's head, which frequently is snuggled in their laps, they talk about their life's journey, freely sharing their joys, sorrows, loves, losses and lessons learned. This is the priceless gift they have given to Andie and me.

Spotlight
Dick, Irma and Vickie

It was a cold wintery day, yet Andie and I were warm and content talking to the residents inside The Forum. We were in our usual place – The Common Area, the central place where residents gathered. I was sitting beside Bev watching her reach for Andie. I took her hand and gently lowered it to Andie's head. Bev is blind and it's difficult for her to find Andie. She just needed a little guidance from me. Once she and Andie connected, her hand stayed close to Andie as she stroked her head. Bev was always excited when Andie and I visited. She would say, "Andie!!!! Where's my Andie?"

This was the beginning of our typical visit; seeking out Bev knowing she was waiting for Andie.

It was while Andie and I were nestled close to Bev's wheelchair that a woman in her mid-fifties walked into the common area and stopped in front us. I looked up at her and saw something familiar in her eyes; a look of confusion, angst and sadness. She hesitated before she walked slowly toward us. She asked if Andie and I ever visited residents in their rooms. I said, "We absolutely do! We love going to their rooms." She hesitated again and then asked if we had time to visit her dad. Immediately, I got up from the floor and looked her square in the face and replied, "How about now?" She said that really anytime we were available would be wonderful. Andie was looking up at me then and as I turned my head towards Andie's eyes, I said, "Let's go sweetie. We have a resident to visit" I made sure to let

Bev know that Andie would be back in a while to spend more time with her.

I introduced myself to the woman and told her Andie was a therapy dog. She told me her name was Vickie. I asked her who we were visiting. She hesitated slightly and in a strained voice said, "My dad." I asked her how long he had been a resident. Vickie was trying to answer in a normal tone, however, I could tell there were so many emotions swirling in her as she answered, "A week. He is recovering from a surgery. We are hoping in a couple of weeks we will be able to take him home. My dad loves dogs. He has always had one." I answered with my heart aching for her, "I hope he goes home even sooner than two weeks."

As we walked into the room, I had a smile on my face as I introduced Andie and me to her father and her mother, who was sitting close to her husband. Vickie introduced her parents to me. She looked at her dad with such heartfelt emotion showing in her eyes and said, "This is my dad, Dick and my mom, Irma."

I walked up to Dick just as he was reaching his hand toward Andie. I whispered in Andie's ears, "Please walk up to Dick and let him touch your head and feel your love, honey." She didn't hesitate. She walked slowly towards his bed and sat down waiting for his hand to touch her head. He was thin and looked weary and listless. Honestly, his eyes brightened when he looked at Andie and slowly let his hand rest on Andie's head.

Vickie began talking about how her dad loved dogs. They had always had a dog growing up. As she was sharing this with me she was looking at her dad with adoring eyes. "Dad, Vickie asked, tell Andie and Marsha about the story of Pachi." Irma looked at her husband as she held his other hand and smiled. "Dick, it is a wonderful story. Please share it."

Dick looked at Vickie, then Irma and finally turned his head toward Andie and me and in a voice that I could barely hear, he began his story.

Pachi was a German Shepard K-9 dog in training. A friend of mine, a policeman, had been working with her. She was a couple of months into her certification and my friend had tried his hardest to get her to the point where she was a certified K-9 dog. He talked to me one day and said, "Dick, I have tried to train Pachi to be a K-9 on the police force, but, honestly, she lacks the focus a K-9 needs when she is out working. Pachi is a good dog. I just don't think she is up to the challenge nor the intensity of what is required in a K-9. I hate to say this, but, I am going to have to release her from the program." I told him that I would take Pachi. My friend finally said that would probably be the best thing for the dog.

Dick paused for a few moments, looked at Irma with a wry smile, swallowed a couple of times and continued his story. "I asked Irma that day if she would like to have another dog in our family." As I was listening, my eyes were on Irma. She clasped her hands around his and kissed them so lovingly. It was like they were sharing this moment; sharing this story as one. Dick looked from Irma back to Andie and me and with all of the love you saw between the two of them, you heard it in the six words he spoke, "I knew she would say yes." My eyes filled with tears as I looked at Irma and Dick. I saw the deep love they felt for each other. I sensed that they could read each other's thoughts. Irma had her eyes locked on Dick's eyes as I waited to hear the rest of the story.

Vickie had been sitting next to Irma this whole time listening with a smile on her face and a powerful love for her father as he shared his story. Vickie gently said, "Dad, share the story about the wasps." Her dad had this faraway look in his eyes as he wrinkled his brows. "Remember, dad, what Pachi did?" Dick slowly shook his head up and down and his lips turned up into a smile. He looked at

Vickie as he began sharing the story she so desperately wanted him to remember.

"I was in the backyard cutting the grass. Irma was at the store and Vickie was on the sun porch playing. The door was open and all of a sudden, Pachi ran out the back to where I was cutting the yard. She was barking and pacing back and forth. She ran back into the house. A few seconds later she ran to the back door again, barking at me. I stopped the mower and ran inside. I couldn't believe what I was seeing. On the sun porch was my little girl waving her hands back and forth and crying her eyes out. There was a wasp's nest in the corner of the ceiling. Pachi was right next to Vickie running around her and biting wasps as they were trying to attack Vicki. Pachi was barking and biting and all the while, the wasps were stinging Pachi on all parts of her body. I scooped up Vickie and we ran outside. Meanwhile, Pachi was fighting off the wasps as they continued to attack her. I got a broom, ran back into the sun porch and knocked down the wasps nest. I slammed that broom around the room killing ever last wasp. It took a long time, but I got them all. I looked over at Pachi as she was lying on the floor half dead. She had been stung so many times that her body began to swell. I called the vet and told him he needed to get over to the house- our dog, Pachi, had been stung by wasps. I was afraid she was as good as dead. Vickie was crying as Irma came into the house and saw the commotion. She wrapped Vickie into her arms, looked at Pachi and started to cry. The vet came and took a look at our dog. He said if she was going to pull through, we needed to keep her in a quiet place and not feed or water her for three days. He said that was the only way she may survive. We checked on Pachi a lot over the next three days and finally she started to get up and walk around. By the fourth day, she was pretty much back to her old self."

Vickie said to her dad, "She should have been a K-9 dog. She had the focus and the intensity that your policeman friend said was needed to be certified. She showed us how much she loved us, Dad!"

Dick looked at Vickie for a long time shaking his head in agreement. I am sure he was remembering that time and remembering what Pachi had done to save his little girl's life.

I had noticed throughout the story of Pachi Dick shared with Andie and me, his words became more clear and easier to understand and he had become more lucid; not as lethargic and listless as when I had first walked into his room.

At this point, Andie was laying down with her head close to the bed and her eyes closed as she was relaxing listening to our conversation.

As I looked at Irma and Dick, I asked "How long have you two been married?" Well, it was almost like this huge sunbeam illuminated the room because of the smiles I saw beaming ear to ear from Irma, Dick and Vickie! Irma said, "63 years." "Wow, how wonderful is that!! I said, so, tell me how you met"

Dick was quick to share their story. "We were sixteen years old. She and I didn't really know each other that well, but I sure thought she was cute. She was giving a speech one day in class and I decided she might notice me if I sat on the front row. I listened to her speech and thought she did a great job. In fact, I walked up to her afterwards and said what a good job she had done. She was pretty shy and so was I so that was about all that was said. A few days later, I was in the library and saw Irma. She was reading a book about horses" Irma chimed in at that point, "I used to ride horses." About that time, a friend of Dick's walked up to him in the library and knew he was interested in Irma. He said I'll bet you five bucks you can't get her to go out with you." Dick suddenly had this glean in his eyes when he said, "I told my friend, you're on!" I walked up to Irma and asked her if she'd like to go horseback riding. She said yes! Now, you know, I had never been on a horse in my life! I took her to these stables and we mounted the horses and took off. We had been riding for about an hour when we stopped by this pond so the horses could drink some water. When they were done, I said, Okay, let's head back. I started walking my horse, turned around to make sure Irma was following and her horse was still standing in the pond. I went back and asked Irma what was wrong. She said that her horse wouldn't budge from the pond. We tried and tried to get that horse to walk out of the pond and he was so stubborn! I was getting nervous so I told Irma I would be back. I would go for help to get this horse to move! I rode back to the stable as fast as I could and told the folks we needed help. It wasn't but two minutes later; I heard the sound of horse's hooves coming from behind. I turned to look and by golly, there was Irma and that stubborn horse coming towards me. Irma had this grin on her face as she came up next to me and said, Dick, I just needed to be a little patient. It all worked out." You know, I never did get on a horse again, but I got Irma!"

It was Vickie I was looking at as Dick finished his story. She had tears welling up in her eyes as she looked at her parents. I looked at her and said, "Vickie, their story is like a fairytale. You are so lucky to have parents that have loved each other for so long." Vickie gave me this look that revealed her love and respect for her parents and said, "I know how lucky I am. There aren't too many of my friends who can say that about their parents. I cherish what I have and I never forget it. Never!"

The physical therapist walked in the room just then. She said, "Well, it's time for your therapy, Dick."

I knew it was time for me to leave. Andie and I got up and before we left, I looked at the three people that I had just spent 45 minutes with and said, "We so enjoyed visiting with you. Thank you for sharing your stories." In unison, Dick, Irma and Vickie told us how much our visit had meant to them. I could hear this message came from their hearts.

I walked back to the common area with love in my heart. I had just spent 45 minutes with three people that had impacted my life. When Vickie had first approached Andie and me her familiar look of confusion, angst and sadness had reminded me of when my mother was in The Forum. She was recovering from a bout of pneumonia and had atrophied. She was there to build her strength back so she, too, could move back to her home. My feelings at that time matched what Vickie was experiencing. There were a range of emotions swirling in my body about my mother, her ability to truly live at home and the thought that she may have to move from where she and my dad had lived for fifty six years and raised three children to a facility with a room that held two beds; one for each patient. My heart went out to Vickie because I had been there, lived through it and had felt those agonizing emotions about the situation. That day I benefited from our visit with those three special people. I only hoped that Andie and I had helped them in their journey.

Spotlight
The Common Area

I tied the Pets for Life bandana around Andie's neck as I always did before going to The Forum for our weekly visit. I looked in her eyes and said, "Okay, honey, we're going to work now!" Honestly, she seemed to know what that meant when I secured that bandana around her neck.

We walked through the front door, took the elevator up to the second floor and proceeded to the common area as was our normal routine. This is where many of the residents gathered during the day. They would wake from a long night's sleep, shake the cobwebs from their head and ease into their wheelchairs or reach for their walker. Their daily destination was the same; their ritual never altered. The common area was their place to settle in for the duration of the day.

The residents came from all walks of life. They each experienced different illnesses. They were there for a reason: a reason that didn't agree with some. Others resolved themselves to their situation. They were contained in a room they either shared with a bed mate or had a single room. Nevertheless, they were all there day in and day out waiting, hoping, praying that things would change. Most times things stayed the same no matter how much or how hard they wished and prayed otherwise.

Andie and I always visited the common area first. It was where many of the residents "hung out" for the day. We would see the "usual's" biding their time. Some residents simply sat in their wheelchair and dozed throughout the day, others staring at nothing and most had little interaction with the other residents.

Many times I would look down the two hallways that led to the bedrooms and would often see residents in their wheelchair "walking" up the hallway by pushing one foot and then another foot in front of them slowly scooting towards the common area. There were times when those residents would stop to rest. It was a long hallway and they simply didn't have the strength to make it without resting. There were times when it took them over an hour to reach their destination.

I would take Andie to those residents and ask if they would like to pet her. Many of the residents loved the attention she gave them. We would sit with that resident as he or she reached out to touch Andie and stroke her head or body. I would talk with them while they rested with Andie by their side. There was a reason why I did this. It pained me to see their struggle and determination to move down the hallway to the common area. I wanted to give them an excuse to stop and rest.

Over the months that Andie and I had been visiting the residents, I continued to notice the fortitude and conviction of the residents who strove to leave their room and slowly move toward the common area. As I said, for some residents it was a slow methodical process to move down the hallway to the common area. In the end, no matter how long it took them to arrive at the common area which meant from ten minutes to sometimes one hour they made it. They succeeded in accomplishing their goal!

I thought about what I had witnessed every week when Andie and I arrived at The Forum. I saw the strength, the willingness and the need for those people who were sequestered in their respective rooms to have the need and want to be amongst people. I saw the desire that drove them to venture down the long hallway, no matter what it took and the means to do it, to arrive at that common area.

In the end, when they arrived, it mattered not that they interacted with one another. It was the simple pleasure of being around living people congregating together. Were there discussions and conversations taking place when they finally met? No, very little of that took place. Was there a gentle touch to another person? No, that did not happen. No, only the need to know that there was life and people living and that they were among that group. They were breathing, eating and enjoying this life on earth, whatever living on life was defined for the individual. Andie and I saw that and understood the value that each of those residents felt about being alive.

I reflected on my own life and the ease of walking or driving to someone's home not even thinking about the struggles of doing that very thing of simply walking down a hallway to meet with someone. Andie's and my weekly visits became that much more important to us because of what we saw in those residents who thrived to live their lives. What a joy for Andie and me to appreciate through the eyes of those residents the love of life.

Andie's Health

Andie and I woke up one morning and it was different. She and I cuddled together and loved on each other as we always had. We kissed and cuddled together like usual. When she got out of the bed, she stumbled and fell. It scared me! I was frightened by her fall. It was so unusual for her.

As she was lying on the floor next to the bed, I immediately lay down next to her and asked her how she was. How strange for her to fall down off of the bed. I was so concerned about her that I grabbed and held her for the longest time. I asked her how she felt; even though I knew she couldn't tell me. She was lethargic and quiet. I didn't move her. I just lay next to her wondering what the problem was with her body. She was struggling trying to lift her legs. This had never happened before. She had always been a vibrant dog. There had never been an issue with her legs. Today was very different. She was not responding. She whimpered and cried as I tried to lift her up to the bed.

I said, "Andie girl, what is the matter? What can I do to make you feel better?" She continued to whimper to a point where I knew I needed to call the veterinarian. When I spoke with him, he told me to bring her in. I immediately put her in the car and drove her over to his office. I gently lifted her out of the car and we slowly walked into the office for the vet to examine her.

The vet was waiting for us. He took Andie back to the examination room to do some tests to see what was causing her such pain. I paced the floor in the waiting room for over an hour until the vet came out to talk with me. "Marsha, Andie has severe arthritis. We are giving her medication to help with her condition," he said. "Just know that she is in pain at the moment, but with the medication, she will feel relief soon." I was relieved to hear that there was something that could be done to help her. I had been so nervous, so beside myself thinking about her suffering. Never had I felt such fear as I had that morning when I woke up to Andie's condition. I thought about what I would ever do if anything happened to her. What would I do? I just couldn't think about that; it was too much. She had been the one to help relieve me of that heavy grieving after Mom died. She was my life. She was my love. After the death of my Mom, Andie had become an even greater part of my life. She truly was my life. I couldn't think about if anything ever happened to her. My only thought was making sure she was going to be okay. I wanted to be able to take her home and care for her. That was my only wish.

I lifted Andie into the car and made sure she was comfortable in the passenger's seat. I put the seatbelt around her. I had never done that before, but now I was so worried, I wanted to make sure she was secure when we left the vet's office to drive home. I continually glanced over at her as we drove home to make sure she was comfortable; to make sure she was alive and well. She looked tired. Of course, she was tired. She had a long day beginning with that morning when she woke up and fell out of bed.

When we arrived home, I gently picked her up and put her down on the ground. She was wobbly, but was able to slowly walk into the house. Once we were inside, I picked her up again and put her on the bed. She needed rest. The vet had told me to keep her quiet and to continually give her the medication he had prescribed. He said that I should see a noticeable improvement in her condition over the next couple of days.

I spent all of my time with Andie over the next several days to make sure the medication was working and her condition was improving. It was noticeable that she was feeling better. She had a lighter step in her walk as she strolled around the house. I decided to test out walking her down the street. When I got the leash out, Andie was excited. She even jumped up and down signaling that she was ready to go visit her dog friends on a walk in our neighborhood.

I put the leash on and she scratched at the front door telling me, "Mommy, let's go for a walk NOW!" We walked out the door and took a pleasant stroll down the street. We ran into many of Andie's dog friends and she was so excited to see them that her tail wagged all the way down the street. We stopped frequently for my little girl to sniff and love on her furry friends she had not seen for a few days.

I decided it was time to head back home. The sun was setting and Andie was tiring as we walked back. When we walked into the house, I took her leash off and she looked up to me with those vibrant brown eyes and I could tell she was feeling better. My heart felt good because she was healing. My prayers had been answered. She was on the mend, I was so relieved!

Andie's Last Visit to the Forum

Although Andie was better, I knew it was time that we ended our weekly visits to The Forum. I was reluctant to call the Director of Pets for Life because it was the ending of a beautiful time that Andie and I had experienced together as a therapy team. Over the last fourteen months, I'd looked forward to our Thursday afternoons where we would walk through the doors of The Forum to visit with the residents. They had become very accustomed to our visits. It was so delightful every time we walked in because the residents were waiting for us, always!

Whether they were in wheelchairs, walkers or able to walk on their own, they welcomed us with kisses and hugs. It had been an incredible experience for Andie and me to spend time with the lovely residents. Some of the residents had family and friends that visited them, yet, many residents were alone with no one but the staff of The Forum to care for and love them.

Those residents especially loved our visits. It gave them something to look forward to. It gave them a purpose. Even though their journey in life was at the ending stage, they still had so much to offer and they still had life to live. Andie and I helped them with living their life and giving them the love and care that they deserved. It was Andie they wanted to see. It was Andie they wanted to pet, love and talk to. I was in the background. After they loved on Andie, I began asking them questions about how they were feeling, about their own life's journey. Even though Andie was the primary reason they welcomed us, in the end, I was the one who asked the questions and discovered the joys and sorrows of their lives. As Andie lay next to each resident, I was the one talking with them and finding out about their lives.

Andie was the primary focus for the residents, yet, I was the one who found out about their lives. We were a good team. For the last fourteen months, the residents had made an impact on our lives. I only hoped that we had made an impact on them.

I spoke to the Director of Pets for Life, Debra and told her Andie's issues with her arthritis. We had loved our time together at The Forum, but it was too difficult for Andie to walk the halls and greet the residents. She understood and said that she would talk with the Director of The Forum, Steve, about this.

The next week, the Director for Pets for Life called and said that she had spoken to the Director of the Forum. He had been so sad by the news and was concerned about Andie. He went on to say how much Andie had made an impact on the residents. They looked forward to Thursday afternoons when Andie would come for her visit. The Forum Director wanted to have a good bye party for Andie to honor her for what joy she had brought to the residents.

I was in awe of this news! Of course, we'd love to be there! That next Thursday afternoon, I tied Andie's Pets For Life bandana around her neck, walked her out to the car and carefully lifted her in because she had been having some issues with her arthritis that day. I told her that we were going to visit the residents at The Forum. She looked at me with her beautiful brown eyes and a smile on her face. She knew where we were going and she was excited!

When we pulled into the parking lot, Andie's tail was wagging right and left! Her arthritis didn't stop her from looking forward to seeing the residents. I lifted her out of the car and we slowly walked through the doors of The Forum, like we had done so many times before. This time was the last time.

As we entered, all of the residents were waiting for us. The residents in their wheelchairs, the one's with their walkers, the others able to walk on their own, were all waiting for us in the common area.

There were balloons and streamers and a banner that said "We love you Andie!"

My heart melted by the love they showed Andie! Each resident individually walked up to Andie, gave her a kiss or a pet on her head and told her how much they would miss her. Andie simply sat down on the floor and let them come to her. They gave her a box of dog bones as a gift from all of the residents. We spent an hour with all of them.

I felt so honored that they loved Andie this much that they wanted to tell her and show her how she had impacted their lives. Little did they know that they had impacted my life as much if not more.

After the celebration, I walked up to each resident and shared with them how much it had meant to Andie and me to be a part of their lives. I wished them well on their journey.

Now, Andie and I were on our own journey.

Andie and Me

Andie and I spent most of the next fourteen months staying close to home. She was still on arthritis medication. It seemed to work most of the time, however, there were some days where she was so stiff in her legs that she would walk about three feet and then lay down to rest. It was so unsettling to see my little girl aging. I called the vet and asked him if there was anything else besides medication we could try on Andie to relieve her of her aching and stiffness. He said that he had recently become a certified acupuncturist and thought that by giving Andie treatments would reduce the inflammation and relieve her stiffness. I told him I was all for that; anything to help her live life without pain.

We went to see the vet the next day and I decided to wait while he conducted the acupuncture treatment. About an hour later, he brought Andie out to the waiting room where I had been sitting anxiously. He said that the treatment went well. He asked me to keep a close eye on Andie the next couple of days to see if there was a noticeable improvement in her.

When we got home, she was tired from the treatment so I lay down on the sofa and she slowly walked up and lay next to me on the floor. I reached my hand down and gently stroked her head and rubbed her ears. I said a prayer that I hoped God would hear. I prayed for my sweet little girl to be relieved of her pain. She had never in her life been a burden. She had never shown any temper nor lashed out at any dogs or humans. She truly had always been a gentle, loving dog so willing to give herself to others.

Is there a perfect dog? I am sure if I talked to other dog owners, they would say they had the perfect dog. I am here to say that Andie was definitely THE perfect dog, at least in my eyes. She had always wanted to please and love others. She had loved Meema to the moon and back. It was evident every day that she had been with her. They had been inseparable. The love between them was visible to anyone who was around them. She loved the residents at The Forum. The greetings that we heard every time we walked through the doors was of the residents saying their Hellos and slowly shuffling over to Andie excited to give her a kiss. The walks we took down the street were always filled with Andie's furry friends stopping and having her love on them. Yes, Andie was my perfect dog.

As I was thinking about Andie, I looked down at my girl whose eyes were closed and her snoring was soft and sweet. She was twitching and her legs looked like she was running probably having a dream about chasing a squirrel. In her more youthful days, she chased squirrels until they ran up a tree to escape. She would run up and down the dog park for hours just loving the wind in her face. She was always so active, so vibrant and so healthy.

Now, her legs were arthritic and her gait was slow. I am sure in her dreams she was still that young dog always ready to play, run and jump. I couldn't help but pause for a moment and wish all of those days back. Those beautiful times when together we would be filled with energy and able to walk for miles without getting winded. Oh my, how I did so wish for time to turn back; to when I first laid eyes on the brown ball of fur with the big brown eyes that looked into my heart. That day began my most precious journey in life because of Andie. My life changed that day for the better.

Now, we were still on our journey together. We spent all of our time together. Andie still got excited when I asked, "Do you want to go for a walk, Andie girl?" She so wanted to walk, it's just that her legs would only take her so far and she would have to rest for a while.

I had noticed over the last fourteen months that our walks were shorter, her breathe was more labored when we had gone just four houses down the street. I knew part of it was her arthritis, but I also knew it was her age. She was now twelve years old. She had gray whiskers and even grayer eyebrows that were so pronounced. She had grown into a beautiful older dog that still had a young heart.

We spent much of our time lying on the bed. For years Andie would effortlessly leap on the bed. Now I had to lift her up to put her on the bed. This became our life. Yes, we went out for our short walks, but mostly we lived a quiet life in the house. We were never more than a couple of feet from each other. We liked it that way. Our world was in the house and with each other. I didn't want to socialize with my friends at that time in my life because Andie needed me. Honestly, it was me who needed Andie the most. Every day, I woke up to my sweet little girl and prayed all would be well. Some days were good and she had a spring in her steps. Those days were precious to me. I caught a glimpse of that young dog bursting with energy. Other days, I saw my little girl struggling to walk. My heart ached as I heard her wince with pain because of her arthritis. Those days I laid close by her side. She knew I loved her.

Oh, the journey of life. It can be absolutely beautiful and filled with waking up in the mornings and looking forward to what exciting things would happen that day. Andie and I had experienced those wonderful times together for twelve years. Now, she was on the last part of her life's journey. I knew it, but didn't want to accept it. It was too hard to imagine what my life would be like without Andie. All I wanted to do was be there with her, love her all of the time and pray her life's journey would be extended for a long time. Is that too much to ask? My mom used to say, "Marsha, we are not going to live forever. It is the cycle of life. You have to know that. You have to accept that there is a beginning and an ending to life." Remembering those words she spoke to me so many times still didn't relieve the pain in my heart.

When Mom died, a part of me died. I had wanted her to live forever. Call it selfishness; call it not wanting to lose someone you love so much. Mom had always been there for me. We had been there for each other, especially after Dad died. Our relationship grew even closer because she needed me and I, so needed her. I realized after Dad died that Mom was still alive. I made a promise to myself that I would treasure every moment, every second of my time with Mom. I didn't want to have any regrets when she died thinking, oh, I should have spent more time with her. I should have called her more often.

I upheld my promise and didn't have any regrets about focusing my life on Mom. She and I spent the next thirteen years loving each other, having fun and living our lives together. When she died, even though I had no regrets, I felt lost because I couldn't call her, I couldn't see her, I couldn't hug her and tell her how much I loved her.

That was my fear with Andie. She and I had been together for so many years. The first seven years, it had been Meema, Andie and me. We had been inseparable. It was a wonderful time in my life because I had Meema and Andie. We built a life together and that life was filled with joy, love, happiness and a sense of security. After Mom died, it took Andie and me a long time to adjust to our continued journey in life without Meema. Both of us had grieved and together we helped each other through that grief. My fear was when I would lose Andie. She was my life. Without her, it scared me to think what my life's journey would be.

So, I continued to pray and hope Andie's journey would continue on forever. Perhaps I wasn't thinking realistically. I didn't want to think about it at all, but those thoughts crept into my mind as I watched my sweet little girl's health decline. I continued to pray for her. I prayed for me as well. I needed to be emotionally strong. I needed to be aware of what was happening with Andie. I couldn't bury my head in the sand. I needed to see clearly and remember Mom's words about the cycle of life. Oh, it was so difficult to do. I wished I could talk to my Mom about how I was feeling. Maybe she knew; maybe she was listening to me; maybe she was sitting next to me holding my hand telling me everything was going to be alright. I felt Mom's presence. She was there.

The Struggle

Over the past two months, Andie was weakening. It was on a Saturday morning when she woke up and stumbled into the kitchen and had a violent bout of vomiting. She was so embarrassed and scared. I could see it in her eyes. She scratched on the door to go outside and I immediately let her out.

I flew outside to find out how she was doing. She was lying under the maple tree and was quiet. I knew something was wrong, but was unclear about what was happening.

I gently walked her back into the house, went out to my car and picked her up and put her in the backseat. I wanted to take her to my dear friend, Cindy's house to hear her thoughts on what might be going on with Andie. When I arrived, Andie was able to slowly get out of the backseat of the car and walk into her home.

I explained what had happened and because of their long term relationship with Andie, they looked at her and said that she seemed to be listless and a bit gaunt in the face. We all agreed I needed to call the vet and take her in that day to get her checked. I was so anxious because of the severity of the vomiting and my friend's feedback about her listlessness and the weary look on her face scared me. I know it may sound selfish, but I wanted Andie to be a part of my life for many more years to come.

After calling the vet and telling him I was bringing Andie over to get her checked out, I felt anxious throughout my entire drive over there. Andie was lying in the back laying quietly and staring at me the whole drive over. I just didn't know what was wrong and that was the most worrisome part of this entire experience.

We arrived at the vet and I took Andie into the vet's office. The vet was waiting for me. He said he wanted to examine her and do some blood tests on her. Because it was a Saturday, she would have to stay over the weekend, so I wouldn't see her nor would I know anything about the blood tests until Monday.

It was a long weekend for me. I left the vet's office alone. When I arrived at the house, I walked into silence; a silence I wasn't used to. There was no barking; there was no Andie running to greet me; there was no Andie. I sat down on the floor and cried. I cried for the hurt my little girl was feeling. I cried for the uncertainty about what I would find out with the blood test results. I cried for the silence in the house. I just cried because of the love I felt for my little girl who was my world; my life; my love. She had to be at the vet through the weekend and without me to love her and without her to love me. It was our relationship that we had created, cultivated and nurtured over the past twelve and one-half years that made us one unit; a partnership. We relied on each other, looked out for each other and loved each other to the moon and back. It wasn't a one way relationship. My friends always told me that Andie and I had a symbiotic relationship like nothing they had ever seen before. We were a team. Where I went, Andie was always with me. You could see how we loved each other. It was so unique. I had dedicated my life to Andie and she was loyal, loving and dedicated to me as well. If you saw me, you saw Andie with me. We were never apart. I know that may sound too much, but when you find your true companion, then you take full advantage of building that relationship, loving each other and enjoying life together. That was our life together and it worked beautifully.

Monday morning couldn't come soon enough. I had a restless night wondering what the vet had found with the blood test results. I walked in at 8:01, a minute after the office opened. Since the staff had known Andie I for over twelve years, they were not surprised to see me immediately after the office opened.

I walked up to the desk and asked if the doctor was in. They said he was with a patient and would be out in about fifteen minutes. I sat down on the bench and wrung my hands together worried about what to anticipate what the vet was going to share with me about Andie's blood results. I was scared. I was really scared because I didn't want to hear bad news. Andie was my life. I just couldn't imagine living life without her. I just kept doing self-talk and reassuring myself that the news would be good and that I would put Andie in the car, drive home to our house and give her a big kiss and love on her.

It took thirty minutes until the vet was finally free. He sat down with me and said, "Andie's blood tests on her kidneys show a high level of BUN. I asked him what that meant. He said that the normal BUN is 25 and hers was 82. That meant that her kidneys were in danger. He said that she needed to be hydrated. He recommended that they keep her at the vet and give her 400 CCs of saline daily for seven days. He just to make sure that her BUN stabilized to 25 from where it was at the point at 82.

I asked him if she was going to be okay. He said that he needed to monitor the progress of the saline treatments over the next seven days.

I had this gut wrenching feeling in my stomach when I was listening to his words. My little Andie was suffering and needed treatment for the next seven days. I knew she was in good care but I wouldn't be with Andie for those seven days. My feelings were spewing all over the place because I wasn't sure what the end result would be.

When I arrived home that evening, I walked in to an empty house again. There was not one sound; not one bark. Andie was not there. She was over at the vet clinic being taken care of. It was a weird feeling walking into my house without Andie greeting me. I had a restless night sleeping because Andie and I used to sleep together.

Without her lying next to me, I felt there was someone missing. She was missing. I was lonely without her and felt there was such a void without her cuddling next to me. I prayed to God that everything would be fine with her. I prayed to God that Andie would be with me for a long time. I prayed to God all night long.

The vet called the next day and told me that Andie's BUN was still high. He wanted to talk with me in person. I told him I would be there in ten minutes! As I walked in to the vet clinic, the doctor was waiting for me. He took me into a small room and reluctantly told me that he had done everything he could to help Andie. Her BUN was still high and he said that her kidneys were compromised. I sat there listening to him as tears streamed down my face. "What do we do now, Doctor?" I said in a whisper. "You take her home and just love her, Marsha. She still as some fight left in her. Just love her. She will let you know when it is time." he said with a heartfelt tone. The words were so hard to hear. My heart felt like it had stopped after he told me to just love her and that she would let me know when it was time. Oh God, I didn't want it to be time! I never wanted it to be that time when I would have to let my Andie go!

He went to get Andie and as she slowly walked towards me, I knelt down and wrapped my arms around her and told her again and again how much I loved her. I looked into the beautiful brown eyes that had captured my heart when I first saw her and just cried. She and I were going to go home and love on each other. I was going to savor every minute with my little girl.

A week had gone by since I had picked Andie up from the vet. I had spent all of my time just being with Andie. She seemed tired yet she also seemed content being at home with me. I relished our time together. I kept praying to God that he would work miracles and heal Andie.

Andie's Final Journey

It was a struggle this morning. Andie woke up at 2 a.m. I heard a bark from far off in the family room. I immediately woke up and wandered around the house until I found her lying near the fireplace. I said, "Do you need to go outside, little girl?" She slowly got up on her four paws and walked over to the door. I opened it and let her outside. I sat on the steps to the outside and watched and waited for her. She sat underneath the tree for a good while and finally decided to come inside.

I lifted her back into bed with me and she and I slept until 6:20 a.m. My sister called because she and her husband were about ready to board for their cruise. I told my sister that Andie seemed to be doing okay. She was resting. My sister and I spoke for another twenty minutes and then I hung up and snuggled up to Andie, who was fast asleep by my side.

At 8:00 a.m., I woke up and cuddled on Andie. As usual, I wrapped my body around hers and kissed on her ears, her eyes, and her head; always snuggling as closely together so we could touch each other knowing that we were together. She was my joy as I was hers. That had been our routine for years and one that we relished together: just knowing that we were one together.

I spent two hours enjoying our routine yet, something had changed in Andie. She wasn't as excited or as responsive to my loving as she usually had been. She seemed tired, listless and unresponsive. I kept telling her how much I loved her, how much she meant to me (the world!) and that she was and had been the very best loving dog I had the privilege of spending my days and life with.

I called my dearest friend, Cindy, and asked if she could come over to my house because I wanted her opinion about what decision I needed to make about Andie's health. She was over in less than fifteen minutes. She walked in and bent down to pet Andie. She had known Andie since she was a puppy. In fact, it was two weeks earlier and I took Andie out to Cindy's house. Cindy commented on the change in Andie, then. She said her face looked thinner and gaunt. She said that she was concerned with her health. Now, two weeks later, Cindy, is in my house looking at Andie and then turns towards me and says, "Marsha, she looks tired. You don't want her to get to a point where she is so compromised that you have to do something immediately. You want her to die with dignity and grace. You want her to be put down when she is not in severe pain and agony.

My eyes teared up as I heard her words. I sat down next to Andie and wrapped my arms around her and kissed her head, her nose and whispered in her ear, "I love you Andie girl. I want to do what is best for you and not have you suffer."

I then told Cindy I was going to call the vet and tell him we were going to bring her in and have her put down. After that difficult phone call, we put Andie in the car and drove to the vet's office. All the way there, I held Andie and told her again and again how much I loved her and how she had brought so much joy and happiness to my life. She was my life!

As we walked into the vet's office, my heart was pounding, my legs shaking and my breathing was labored. I felt like I was playing God and making a decision that would end in death. I so didn't want to do this. I was torn between being selfish and wanting Andie to stay with me for more days and weeks because of the love I felt for her or to give her the kind of farewell that was wrapped with love, dignity and grace.

Cindy and I spoke to the vet and I asked, "Do you think it really is time to put her down?" His reply was, "Over the past several months, I have seen a decline in Andie. Her kidneys and intestines are compromised, she has lost a significant amount of weight and she is losing muscle mass. She hasn't had the zest and excitement in her that I used to see. If you don't do this today, there will be a good day she has, then a couple of bad days, then another good day followed by several bad days. I believe she is tired. She loves you so much, Marsha, and she is trying her hardest to stay alive for you. You are asking my opinion and the answer is I believe you need to put her down. I don't and you don't want her to get to a point where it is a severe situation where she is in excruciating pain and suffering before you put her down."

I felt like I couldn't breathe. I felt like my life was at a standstill because I was going to miss her in so many ways; the way she would always greet me at the door wagging her tail and loving on me, our routine of cuddling in the morning on the bed and having me kiss her and love on her before the day started, the excitement of going for our walks to meet her dog friends along our path, the hundreds of ways we touched and loved one another and other people throughout our lifetime with hikes, visiting with the residents as a therapy team at the assisted living facility and simply the enjoyment of quiet time together laying side by side as I read and she chewed on her favorite treat. The memories are countless and always will be close to my heart.

I looked at Cindy and then my eyes focused on the vet. The words were so hard to say, yet, I knew in my heart they were the right words, "I love Andie and I do want her to die with grace and dignity. So, I believe today is that day for her to cross over the rainbow bridge."

We went into a private room and the vet was very caring as he explained the procedure of first giving her a sedative to calm her down, then injecting her with the serum that would end her pain. I lay next to her and the vet injected her with the sedative. My vet had known Andie since she was six weeks old and he was equally invested in her and cared a great deal for her. It was so apparent because he laid down on the other side and as he injected the sedative, he spoke to Andie with kinds words coming from a loving heart. Then, he told me he was going to inject the serum that would put her to sleep. As he did it, he touched her, loved her, and softly said the words, "Andie, you have been such a sweet, loving dog. You have been blessed with a good life. I want you to go to heaven and play with the zest and zeal you had in your younger years. Go enjoy and know you are blessed."

He told me when her heart stopped. It had been peaceful. I stayed by her side for quite some time telling her how much I loved her and what joy she had brought to my life. I told her she had brought joy to so many people's lives throughout her journey in life. As tears streamed down my cheeks, I kissed her one last time and said, "We will see each other again, my little Andie girl."

Andie's Inspiration

It was early morning and I was lying in bed thinking about Andie. I thought about our life we had together, the life we had shared with Meema and the journey we had experienced together as a therapy couple. My thoughts were focusing on Andie and truly understanding how she had impacted my life.

Yes, she had entered my life unexpectedly through the article I had read in the Milwaukee Journal about forty-four puppies that had been rescued from an Indian Reservation. The day I read about them changed my life forever without me even knowing that was going to happen. I have heard that you don't choose your dog; instead your dog chooses you for a specific reason. I didn't know that day that I tucked her into my down vest and drove away from the Humane Society that she would teach me many lessons.

She taught me the gift of slowing down and appreciating the people in my life. That was evident with the relationship Meema, Andie and I had together. Yes, my Mom and I had a beautiful relationship prior to Andie entering our lives. We spent time together every day loving and living our lives together. When Andie came into our lives, she brought a joy and a spirit of loving life that inspired Mom and I to rejoice and embrace every day like we had never done before. She taught us true unconditional love through her daily acts of love for both of us.

The many times she would jump out of the car after we pulled into Mom's driveway. She couldn't wait to race into Meema's house knowing that she would receive the love, kisses and hugs from Meema that she always could count on. That didn't just happen. It was Andie who unknowingly and innocently loved Meema and showed her how she felt by opening her heart to her. By doing that, Meema immediately reciprocated. It was because Andie was her guide to understanding how a beautiful animal can show a human being about unconditional love. Andie helped Meema rise above her grief from the loss of Dad and love again! Mom rediscovered herself through Andie. This little brown ball of fur taught Meema how to love again.

Andie taught me the art of listening through our journey as a therapy team. When we visited the residents at The Forum, it was Andie the residents were excited to see, pet and love. I was in the background seeing the exchange between the residents and Andie. It was so obvious that she gave them a gift by just being her; by gently sitting next to each person and allowing them to kiss her, pet her and talk with her about whatever was on their mind. My Andie sat patiently next to them listening to their stories. I learned through Andie the art of truly listening, patience and being engaged with people.

Andie taught me how to love completely. It hadn't occurred to me that over the years I had lived and loved her, she was teaching me every day the meaning of life and loving other people unconditionally. I hadn't realized that she had been my guide, my mentor and my guardian angel.

I thought I had always known the true meaning of what love was; understanding the importance of just sitting with someone and letting them share their story of their life's journey. I realized at that very moment, she had taught me more than I had taught her in her lifetime. How had I missed the lessons she had taught me? How could I have not grasped the beauty she showed me about life and the love of it all?

I thought I had been her guide, her mentor, yet, in the end, I realized she had always been the guide; my guide. It was so eye opening that in the twelve years Andie and I had been together, she had continually made it her mission to teach me about how to live life to its fullest. I was in awe of what I had just discovered. Andie had looked after me the whole time; not me looking after her.

I sat down and looked up to God and to my little girl Andie, who I was hoping was waiting on the Rainbow Bridge for me to finally cross over to heaven. I whispered to my sweet girl, "Thank you for all of the gifts you gave to me. Thank you for showing me unconditional love. Thank you for teaching me the meaning of listening, caring and loving all of the people in my life. I will always remember your lessons, Andie. You are the one who taught me the true meaning of life. Be good my sweet girl and remember to wait for me at the Rainbow Bridge so we can cross over together so we can be there for each other forever.

Thank goodness I found you Andie.

A Note About the Author

Marsha Bjerkan resides in Kansas City and has shared much of her life in the company of dogs. She enjoys a fulfilling career as a leadership trainer and is also the author of Simply a Role Model.

Cover photo: Janet Smith Photos

Printed in the United States
By Bookmasters